TEAM OF DARKNESS

TONY RUGGIERO

Hard Shell Word Factory

This book is dedicated to my loving wife Katie,
and our wonderful daughter, Alexandra,
who were always wondering what I was doing late at night,
and where my mind was the rest of the time,
I love you both so very much.
For Mom and Dad,
I wish you could be here to enjoy this moment with us.
To everyone else who fed my imagination over the years
with the tidbits of information that I twisted
in my own maniacal way into this story,
and so many others.

ISBN: 0-7599-0013-1
Trade Paperback
Published March 2002
© 2002,   Anthony Ruggiero
Ebook ISBN: 0-7599-0011-6
Published February 2002

Hard Shell Word Factory
PO Box 161
Amherst Jct. WI 54407
books@hardshell.com
http://www.hardshell.com
Cover art © 2002 Dirk A. Wolf

PROLOGUE

Present Day

COMMANDER JOHN Reese and the three members of his team disembarked under the cover of darkness on the western side of the island of Jamaica. The deserted beach was known as Bloody Bay. The name was from the island's past, from a time when the bay was a stop for whalers to clean their catches, and the blood tainted the water red.

All four men leapt from the raft. Reese watched as his team dragged the raft ashore and hid it amongst the shore brush. Two days ago, he had studied the pictures from the reconnaissance flight that had shown the beach debris as well as the volcanic rock that comprised most of the shoreline.

All were dressed in black, the exposed areas of skin darkened. No one spoke as they unloaded their waterproof bags and prepared to move out. When the team finished their preparations, Reese moved toward the silent group. Using hand signals he indicated the direction of travel. Each man nodded in acknowledgement. Darkness shrouded their faces and concealed their features. They wore eye devices, similar in appearance to swim goggles, hiding their eyes. Reese was glad he couldn't see their gazes, because if he could, he would see evidence of the hunger that resided within them, a hunger that if not controlled could get him killed.

Reese donned his night vision goggles; the others didn't require visual assistance. They lived in the night. Reese signaled the team and started forward; they moved quickly and quietly behind him.

A few kilometers later, the landscape changed from the deserted shoreline and typical palm trees that languished in the warm tropical air to the outskirts of a small tourist resort. Sand gave way to concrete and stone to accommodate those who paid exorbitant amounts to vacation on the island.

Reese observed his team as they lifted their heads to confirm with their keen senses the smell of civilization. Knowing their capabilities, instead of the clean saltwater scent, they scented the perfumes of human bodies and the abundance of energy that flowed within those bodies, the energy defined as blood. Reese turned his gaze from the men and looked at the unoccupied lounge chairs lined up like soldiers awaiting their assignments. In the red glow of a small light, he studied the map, comparing landmarks in his sight to those on the chart. They were near the objective now.

The others gathered around him. His motions indicated their current location and their next direction. The target was less than a kilometer away. Again they moved out, but now stayed within the shadows, avoiding any light. Reese looked at his illuminated watch and glanced at the black horizon. Everything must go according to plan if they were to make it back in time. He caught concerned glances from the men, which he dispelled with a wave of his black-gloved hand.

There had been no way to resolve the time of the incursion. Their sources confirmed the target would only be here one night before returning to the depths of the Colombian rainforests, and away from their surveillance. To complicate matters, their departure had been delayed until the moon had set. Complete darkness was essential to their success. He was sure they could make it if they stayed focused on the mission and didn't run into any problems.

In minutes, a three-story building loomed out of the darkness, rising up from the volcanic hill just east of the bay where they had landed. Its many lights gave it a ghostly pale white color. A magnificent stairwell led to a large open veranda overlooking the bay, then continued upward for another two stories. Massive stone pillars curved into archways. The home, once the center of a large plantation, now had another use: The headquarters for one of the largest drug-smuggling operations that received and transshipped cocaine from South America to the United States.

As they approached the target, Reese observed the heavily armed guards placed to keep the entire area under surveillance. Not only was the area surrounding the mansion well guarded, it was void of any places to hide. The group stopped at the last piece of cover offered by the landscape, a grouping of shrubs massed with a grove of palm trees. Reese removed his night vision goggles, placing them back into the pouch on his belt, then motioned to his men to indicate assignments. His last signal indicated he would wait here until they neutralized the defenses and signaled all clear.

As Reese finished his instructions, he looked at the hooded men as they removed their goggles; the red illumination of their eyes confirmed their hunger. He searched for some reassurance that they would do their jobs. Andre, Iliga, and Dimitri—The Team of Darkness. His gaze settled on the largest of the group, Dimitri, who amongst his own kind, was the leader. *His own kind.* The words gnawed at Reese's never-subdued intellect for debate. His own kind? What the hell was that? He didn't want to discuss the issue again, especially not now. He locked gazes with Dimitri. Those eyes possessed such darkness within the illuminated spheres they left Reese cold. He was already filled with trepidation for what they planned to do. He quelled his fears and, for a moment, contemplated canceling the mission, but the thought left him. He looked away from the gaze of the man who still remained a mystery. They had passed the point of no return.

The three looked at each other then raised their black-masked faces to the air as if smelling the scent of the foul beast they hunted. Their eyes glowed with the awful red hunger. The realization of found prey after a long hunt and that the kill was near at hand made them restless. Reese watched as they prepared to go to what would surely be their deaths...if they were mortal men. But he was the only mortal, the weak link. His presence was almost a hindrance, but necessary to ensure the team followed orders.

They vanished in a blur; Reese attempted to watch their advance. Using his binoculars, he caught glimpses of shadows moving upon the compound from different angles; knowing that someone who had not been trained in what to look for would not see the momentary shifting of light. But he'd been around the Team of Darkness long enough to know what to look for. Team of Darkness—the code word used for this group. He hadn't used the term for quite a while, not since Commander Scott had used it in identifying the...creatures. Reese remembered the pleasure that Scott exuded when he had coined the term. General Stone, the man responsible for all that had happened from day one, must have approved strongly of its usage, and Scott probably earned a gold star that day.

Returning his thoughts to the present, Reese watched as his team soundlessly immobilized the first set of guards. They flew over barbed wire fences as if their bodies were not subject to the laws of gravity. Areas booby-trapped with devices designed to explode from weight disturbances or from detected body heat, failed to respond as the men made their way toward the mansion. Locked gates and doors were opened without any effort; they had conquered the presumed impenetrable defenses that would have stopped even the most capable military force.

As Reese watched the team reach the entrance of the building, he saw Dimitri give the "wait" hand signal to Andre and Iliga. Reese prepared to move onto the next phase of the mission. He removed his Kevlar vest, keeping only his web belt. The attached pouches held only two items: a remote control and a 9mm handgun with silencer. By the time he finished and looked up, Dimitri had returned and signaled his readiness for Reese to go in.

Dimitri focused on one of the pouches on Reese's belt. Reese saw his preoccupation with the pouch, aware that Dimitri knew that it held the device that controlled the creatures while it was in their keeper's hands. Hands being a relative expression—the device would activate if removed from the body it was keyed to, in this case, Reese's.

Dimitri's gaze drifted from the pouch to Reese's face. Reese detected urgency in his expression instead of the usual calm. Knowing that the next phase would be crucial to the success of the mission, Reese signaled he was ready.

Dimitri escorted him past the downed guards. Approaching the mined and the barbed-wire areas, Dimitri lifted Reese off the ground without difficulty. Although he was probably the only person who understood these creatures, he still marveled at their abilities. He was transported safely and deposited at the entrance where Andre and Iliga waited. Reese nodded thanks to Dimitri who did not respond to the gesture. Ignoring Dimitri's lack of response, Reese motioned for them to follow him.

The interior defenses were minimal, considering the impenetrability of the home, and consisted of a few posted guards who were easily circumvented. According to their intelligence source, in this case the housekeeper whose information had been bought with taxpayer's dollars, indicated that the target would be in the study. Reese stopped his team when he spotted a pair of guards stationed outside of the door. The guards were engaged in some type of card game, their attention focused on the flimsy card table instead of the corridor. Reese knew there was no other means of entry into the room. He signaled to Dimitri to immobilize the guards.

Seconds later, the guards were downed before they had even realized that they were in danger. They weren't killed, but paralyzed. They could not speak or move, and as they laid on the cold marble floor in twisted horror, they watched their two attackers. Reese tried to hide his revulsion, but he knew taking down the guards had excited the team members in an erotic way, feeding the anticipation of the promised feeding.

Reese signaled Dimitri to post one of his team with the two

incapacitated guards while they entered the room. He watched as Dimitri signaled his order to Iliga. He noted that the order was followed by suggestions regarding what could be done with the guards. Reese wished he didn't know what Dimitri had in mind for the men. The signal acknowledged and understood, Reese removed his weapon from its holster and the three entered the room.

The target lounged on the sofa flanked by two young naked women who vied for his attention and distracted him from their entrance. His intensive training took charge before his emotions could register the horror about to be committed; Reese signaled Dimitri and Andre. Now came the tough part, the watching. He was an observer with his own personal window view into hell.

Dimitri and Andre approached slowly, appearing not wanting to rush the moment, but to savor it. One of the women caught their movement and looked in their direction; for several seconds she stared, her mesmerized gaze watching the men dressed in black approach.

Andre separated the women from their target and kept a chokehold on them to keep them quiet. Carlos, a notorious drug overlord of the Colombian cartel, peered at the three men, his facial features contorted in amazement.

"How did you get in here?" he demanded in a thick Spanish accent. "*Protectores! Prisa!*"

He attempted to rise, but his pants around his knees only allowed him to stagger like a drunken man. As his chest rose in obvious preparation to scream, Dimitri backhanded him. He flew several feet in the air and crashed to the floor.

Reese turned away from Dimitri and Andre and the game of cat-and-mouse they played. He checked his watch, and then looked out the large window located behind the sofa. Turning back, he gestured to Dimitri and Andre that they were out of time.

Without warning and in perfect unison, Dimitri used one hand to remove his mask, and his other to remove Andre's revealing their faces and the large metal collars around their necks. Their features reflected a strong Slavic appearance, the dark hair and eyes set into faces that were strong but wrinkled from the ravages of the rough environment of the Balkans. When they opened their mouths, the revealed fangs removed any likeness to humans.

Reese wanted to shout: *Don't do it! Just kill Carlos and get out of here.* They didn't have time to waste if they were going to get out. But he knew any attempts to stop them would be to no avail. His team had been purposely starved for this mission and they had to feed in order to survive. His hand curled around the device in the pouch, but he let go and let his hand fall to his side. They were safe: No one had shouted and alarms were silent. If he was going to get away, he needed them. His only choice was to watch the carnage and hope it was over quickly.

Andre, who held the two women, bit into the neck of one, slashing the flesh in a wild frenzy, and drinking deeply. The other woman struggled to cry out as she watched the gruesome act, but his hold was too powerful leaving her only the choice of closing her eyes. Finished with the one, he released his sold and she slumped to the floor. Then he turned toward the other and repeated the gruesome act.

Carlos, the Colombian, still dazed from his fall, looked on in horror as the creature licked and sucked the fluid from his former paramours. Dimitri approached him, baring his large fangs, lifted him off the ground, gashed the man's neck and drank the blood that flowed from the gaping wound.

Reese tried to block out the sounds, but the slurping of blood and the tearing of flesh echoed in his mind. He pushed aside his feelings of disgust. If they were going to survive, they had to get out of here.

"Dimitri, Andre, we have to go now!" Reese whispered as loud as he dare. "Dawn is coming!"

Both Dimitri and Andre looked up, their faces covered with blood and pieces of flesh. They removed knives from their sheaths on their belts and slit what remained of their victims' throats to make it appear as a typical murder of someone who has crossed another drug cartel, the universal sign of a traitor's punishment. Putting on their dark masks, they exited the room.

Reese, stepping out first, saw that Iliga had carried out the same procedure on the two guards. His face covered with blood, his cheeks flushed with a glow that radiated life.

"Put your hood on," Reese whispered.

Iliga replaced his hood.

Reese looked at three of them. Blood dripped from their mouths, streaked their necks, and wetted their clothing. His gaze centered on Dimitri, demanding an explanation.

"Why the women?" asked Reese in a soft demanding voice.

Dimitri's expression said no explanation was required, but still he answered, "Casualties of war."

Andre and Iliga nodded their agreement.

"The mission is accomplished, Commander Reese," added Dimitri. His voice was calm without any hint of remorse.

Reese lowered his head for a moment, shaking it slowly. Should he condemn himself for the acts of cruelty he'd witnessed? He had ignored the signs and that made him an accomplice to the actual events. Shock and disbelief had drained him. After a few moments, he looked at the Team of Darkness and indicated it was time to return to the beach.

The first signs of a brightening sky showed in the east as they paddled their way toward the gray military ship that waited for them.

"We're not going to make it," said Dimitri.

"Row! You son-of-a-bitch! If you love life as much as you say you do, then paddle! Or do you want to end it? Have you had enough of this madness?"

Dimitri said nothing as he continued to paddle.

"No," Reese continued. "That would be too simple for you, wouldn't it?" Reese stopped paddling and waved his arms at the men standing on the bridge of the ship. "Bring the ship closer and turn it to block the sunlight! Hurry!" he yelled.

The patrol craft moved closer and turned the silhouette of the ship toward the east attempting to block the early morning light. The glaring white letters of PC-1 emblazoned on the forward part of her hull appeared ghostly in the pre-dawn light.

"It appears we may live for a while longer," Dimitri said as shade from the ship's superstructure bathed them in dark gray.

"It appears that way," said Reese. "We need to talk about this madness—"

Reese stopped speaking because they were alongside the ship. He remained in the zodiac raft as the three members of his team scrambled onto the ship and hurried below deck. Finally, Reese came on board as crewmembers pulled in the raft. The ship turned away from the coast and headed out to sea.

The young captain of the ship, a Naval Lieutenant, approached Reese.

"Operation Red Blood accomplished, Commander? " he asked in a serious tone that sounded forced.

Reese turned toward the lieutenant as he pulled the black mask off of his face. "Never mind about my mission, Lieutenant," he barked. "Just get us back to base as soon as possible, and remember, the area where my men are at is not to be entered by anyone except the Navy SEALs in my unit. Got that?"

"Yes sir," the lieutenant answered, apparently surprised by Reese's unexpected abruptness. He returned to the bridge area of the USS Cyclone, a coastal patrol craft that operated with the special warfare units out of Little Creek, Virginia. Reese knew it was time for the captain to give the order, all ahead full, to the officer of the deck.

Reese threw his black hood over the ship's side and into the wake of the patrol craft as it picked up speed. As he watched the water, he drifted off into thoughts of how the hell it had come to all this....

CHAPTER 1

One Year Ago

THE DUTY officer massaged his tired face and ran his hands through his close-cropped hair in between sipping his fifth cup of coffee, as he struggled to stay awake at 0300 in the morning. Captain Block, an Army veteran of five years, had been in Kosovo for more than ten months. He'd spent the past six months at Camp Bondsteel, along with four thousand other servicemen and women. The camp was situated on what had once been farm fields near the town of Urosevac, in the southern region of Kosovo, and was part of the international peacekeeping team, or for the Americans, Task Force Falcon.

Task Force Falcon was responsible for the twenty-three thousand square kilometer American zone, maintaining peace and keeping the Albanians and Serbians from killing each other, and at times, even Albanians from killing Albanians. This equated to approximately three hundred and fifty squad-sized security operations every day.

Block was tired of the bloodshed and ethnic division of this country. With only two months left to his tour, he looked forward to going home. His tour in the Army would be over and he was ready to work at his uncle's car dealership. Soft-spoken, with facial features that made a guy either a minister or a car salesman; his fellow soldiers told him that he had the kind of disposition that would ensure him success in the car business.

Block firmly believed in Murphy's Law: If anything could go wrong with the short time left to his tour, it would. He vowed to be cautious and, if at all possible, not to commit to anything dangerous—if he had a choice in the matter. His time and experience in the military had proven he was not a professional soldier; he didn't have any desire to become one.

Tonight had been quiet. With all assignments completed he had busied himself by catching up on some reading and even managed to write a letter to his mom and dad back home in Seattle. As he licked the envelope's flap, he noticed his burly infantry sergeant, Sergeant

Estefan, come into the central command area. He was not hard to miss. A big man, about six feet in height and 225 pounds, he always had a five o'clock shadow at about one o'clock in the afternoon. His face appeared to be made of solid granite—along with his muscles. Although ominous in appearance, Estefan was a calm person and rarely got upset.

Block noticed Estefan was not alone. An obviously agitated civilian accompanied him. He babbled wildly in a native Slavic tongue, making wild gestures with his arms. His body shook as if he was being shocked with electricity.

Observing the agitated man, Block saw that the man's clothing was worn but clean. He was probably a farmer like the majority of the people in the area. They took pride in their clothing that was sewn by hand to endure years of service required from the hard-working people. The man's face was weathered from spending time in the cold and hot temperatures; the wrinkled lines held permanent locations on his face and made him appear older than he probably was. But his eyes reflected strength, energy, and determination.

He watched as Estefan sat the civilian in a chair, then motioned for him to stay there. Apparently the civilian didn't speak or understand English. The sergeant spoke to a corporal then pointed to the civilian. When Estefan moved away, the corporal remained, watching the civilian. Estefan headed toward Captain Block's office, stopped at the door and knocked. Block waved him in.

"Sir, we might have a problem," said Estefan.

"So I see," said Block indicating the civilian. "What's going on?"

"All I know right now is that he's terrified about something. He ran up to the evening patrol, throwing himself in front of their vehicle, yelling and screaming at them to make them stop. The only thing we could understand was the town's name, Kacianik. He kept repeating it over and over again. I have a interpreter on the way to find out what's going on."

"All right. Let's take a look at him. Bring him in here."

The sergeant motioned for the corporal to bring the civilian into the captain's office. Block reminded himself that part of the responsibility of the peacekeeping forces was to maintain order such as a police force would do. Any incident was investigated if the situation warranted it; unfortunately that was his job as duty officer. Either way it would be recorded into the desk log and forwarded to the Base Commander for review as well as to several agencies in the United States.

As the sergeant, corporal, and civilian entered the captain's office, the civilian surprised them all by lunging toward the captain. He grasped the collar of Block's uniform in his hard weathered hands and spoke hurriedly, spraying spittle onto Block's face. Shocked, Block found himself unable to move. The civilian's hands were like steel, locked onto his clothing and he couldn't budge them. In those seconds, he saw that this man was scared out of his mind. His eyes twitched, revealing blood-lined white backgrounds that contrasted with darting pupils. As he continued to rant, the man's body pulsated with uncontrollable fear.

The sergeant and the corporal managed to pull him away from the captain and forcefully sat him into the chair. They kept their hands clamped over the man's wrists and forearm until he settled down. The sergeant released his grip on the man, giving him a stern look and finger wagging that promised retribution if he tried something like that again. Estefan looked at the corporal to be sure he had the man, when the corporal nodded, Estefan turned toward the captain with a look of disgrace on his face.

"Sorry sir. I never thought he would do that. He caught me off guard."

"It's okay. He caught me off guard, too." Block attempted to catch his breath. "Whatever it is, he's scared out of his mind." Then in a low voice that only the sergeant could hear, " I can almost smell the fear from him." The sergeant nodded.

A knock at the door caused Block to look up. A corporal entered; the name on his uniform indicated that he was Corporal Brosnev. His boyish features made him appear eighteen or nineteen years of age. He was five foot six inches and weighed perhaps one hundred and fifty pounds soaking wet.

"Corporal Brosnev, reporting as ordered for interpreter duties, sir," he said in a voice that reflected a nervous untested youth.

"Come in, Corporal," said Block as he waved him in. "I want you to find out what this civilian is ranting about. He's scared out of his mind."

"Yes sir," the corporal responded and went to where the civilian was being held in the chair. Estefan dismissed the other corporal as Brosnev took the position of holding the man's forearms to the chair.

Block listened as the corporal addressed the civilian in the local Slavic dialect. The man's eyes lit up at the recognition. Another onslaught of words spilled from his lips. Brosnev raised his hands and spoke a few words repeatedly to the civilian that Block assumed was telling him to go slowly so that he could understand what he was trying to say. The only word that was recognizable to him was the repeated mention of the town Kacianik. Block continued to listen and watch as the interpreter questioned the civilian. For several minutes they bantered in what seemed to be an unproductive process.

"What's wrong?" asked Block.

"We're trying to agree on a dialect. Between the provinces of the war torn former republic of Yugoslavia, dialects differ immensely."

After a few more exchanges of words, Brosnev raised his hand indicating for the civilian to stop. He turned to speak with the captain.

"His name is Idriz Lauki," said Brosnev. "He lives in a little village outside the city of Kacianik. He says that he has found people that have been murdered and horribly mutilated."

"Is it more ethnic cleansing?" Block asked in a voice that reflected having seen too much of this already. They found mass graves of bodies from these atrocities almost every other day, and there was no getting use to the sight of civilians killed and piled into hastily dug holes. "Ask him to tell you about the killings."

Brosnev spoke again with Lauki who reacted more strongly to the questions. But as Lauki responded, Brosnev appeared to not understand what the man was saying and the frustration on Lauki's face was evident as the lines in his skin pulled tighter. Brosnev released the hold on him, but Estefan tensed as if there might be another outburst.

"He says," said Brosnev, "he says it was not Serbs or Albanians that did the killing." Brosnev turned back to Lauki and spoke slowly as if clarifying each and every word that he had told him. "He says," Brosnev continued, "there are...creatures that came from the ruins of an old church near his village last night. They came from the ruins and killed two people from his village."

"He can't be using the right word. Hostiles, renegade Serbs, looters...who?" Block asked impatiently.

Brosnev asked Lauki the same questions again. "No sir," Brosnev said. "None of them."

"What then?"

"He says they were creatures. Like vampires. They sucked the blood out of the people," said Brosnev quickly as if he had tasted something he did not like.

"What?" Block was incredulous. "What kind of fools does he think we are to believe that story? Tell him to get the hell out of here and stop wasting our time!"

Brosnev spoke harshly to Lauki telling him what the Captain's reaction was to his statement about the creatures. Block was about to return to his desk when Brosnev spoke again.

"He says he can show us where they are."

"The vampires?" Block said mockingly.

"Both. The bodies of the victims, who are his children, and where the vampires live."

Block looked at Brosnev, then glanced at Lauki and shook his head.

Murphy strikes again.

THE VEHICLE bounced over the rutted road as Captain Block, Sergeant Estefan, Corporal Brosnev, and Idriz Lauki headed for an area located outside of the city of Kacianik. The village, considered part of Kacianik, was less then fifty miles from Camp Bondsteel.

Block, seated up front with the driver Sergeant Estefan, was quiet after receiving a painful dissertation from the base commander of what should and should not go into the desk log report. Colonel Antol had tried to instill upon him that he would remember in the future to be more careful, and as a reminder, he could think about it during his trip in the cold and over the terrible roads to investigate the civilian's claim.

The report from the night before had generated some interest from somewhere in the chain of command. Secure computerized versions were immediately available for review by appropriate levels within the military organization. Block had simply categorized the report as unsubstantiated and refused to investigate the incident based upon the civilian's wild accusations of blood-sucking creatures. Now, less then twenty-four hours later, they were on the way to investigate the absurd claim.

The interpreter, Corporal Brosnev, and Lauki conversed about directions; Brosnev relayed them to Estefan. They had been on the road for two hours averaging a speed of twenty-five to thirty miles per hour because of the poor or non-existent road. Between the bumpy slow ride and the cold, everyone was anxious to get out of the vehicle.

Spring was not anxious to arrive in this mountainous area and the winter was bitter. The roads had been bombed earlier in the vicious air campaign by the allied forces, and repair was slow and tedious hampered by bad weather. Although the bombings had destroyed many areas, the countryside with scattered homes and farms was beautiful and picturesque. Historical landmarks were plentiful in this area. Many soldiers spent what little free time they did have in exploring its landmarks.

"How much further?" Block asked, irritated. He had just smacked his head for the third time on a side support strut of the vehicle.

"Just about there," Brosnev responded as they topped a rise that offered a view of the surrounding area.

Block saw some ruins in the valley below. "Is that it?"

"Yes sir," Brosnev answered after Lauki confirmed the site by pointing at it. Lauki looked up at the sky, his expression tentative and his manner nervous. He spoke to Brosnev in a hurried manner. Brosnev questioned his statement for clarity before he translated it.

"Now what?" Block asked sarcastically. His mood worsened with each passing moment. He was cold, uncomfortable, and still thinking about his dressing down by the Colonel.

"He says we can't stay long because it will be dark soon."

Block uttered a sound of disgust that reflected his frustration with Lauki and his story of vampires. "Go ahead and take a quick look-see and get back. We've wasted enough time," Block answered as the vehicle stopped about thirty yards from the ruins. He was certain they wouldn't find anything; he saw no point in climbing over rocks and tramping around anymore than was necessary. Knowing Murphy's Law, he would probably fall and break an ankle.

Lauki jumped out and ran toward the first outcropping of standing walls; he was screaming. Estefan and Brosnev jumped out of the vehicle and raced after him. Block stepped out of the vehicle, but he did not move. His head throbbed with a headache from the rough ride.

"Let me know if there is anything," Block called to Estefan. He lit a cigarette as he resigned himself to being part of a wild goose chase.

AS ESTEFAN and Brosnev turned the corner, they stopped. Lauki kneeled at two bodies on the dirt floor, moaning and crying out the names of his daughters.

"Damn," Brosnev whispered.

"Easy Brosnev," said Estefan as he clasped Brosnev's shoulder. "Start taking notes about the scene."

Brosnev retrieved a notepad from his inner pocket with a shaky hand and started writing. Estefan moved closer to examine the bodies. His previous assignment had been with the Mortuary Corps and he had assisted with autopsies during the Gulf War.

"My guess for their ages is nine and eleven. You can confirm that with Lauki later. They appear to have been dead for about two days. But the low temperatures may have prevented any serious decomposition."

"I don't see any obvious wounds, or any blood on the ground around them, maybe they were killed somewhere else and dumped here."

Lauki screamed at Estefan and hugged the stiff and pale body of the younger girl.

"He says look at their necks," translated Brosnev.

Estefan looked at the girl's neck and saw two puncture wounds that had been hidden by the girl's long dark hair.

"There are small punctures, maybe a quarter of an inch in diameter and spaced apart about two inches."

Lauki sobbing, again called to Estefan, then showed him the wounds on the other girl. The marks looked identical. Lauki's voice was weak but he managed to mutter some words to Brosnev.

"That is where the creatures bit into them and sucked their blood," Brosnev said. Estefan stared at the girls then at their father.

"The girls look pale, much paler then the ones I saw in the Gulf, but I'm not the expert in these types of medical matters. For all I know, some snake could have bitten them or the cold turned them to their current color condition." Estefan turned away from the bodies and looked at Brosnev.

"Ask him if he would mind if we took them back to the Camp to have an autopsy performed."

Brosnev relayed the information. Lauki wiped the tears streaming down his face, then nodded his approval and added some other comments.

"He agrees, but he says we must leave quickly. It will be dark soon and this is not a safe place."

"Why not?" Estefan asked.

"He says the creatures live in the old catacombs underneath here." Brosnev pointed toward the ground.

"I don't know what to make of any of this. Dead children and stories of vampires. It's beginning to sound like a horror movie. The bodies need to be examined by a doctor or other expert who can determine the cause of their deaths."

Estefan looked at the children, Lauki, then Brosnev. "Come on. Give me a hand covering up the bodies and putting them in the vehicle," he said. Estefan and Brosnev removed folded emergency blankets from the pouches attached to their web belts.

Lauki removed a bottle of dark liquid from inside his coat and began splashing its contents on all of them.

"What the hell is that? Oh man, it stinks!" Estefan gestured to Lauki to stop. Brosnev wiped droplets from his face as he spoke to Lauki. Words were quickly exchanged.

"He says it will ward off the creatures. It's poison he's made from a recipe passed down through his family over many generations."

"If it wards off the creatures, why didn't it save his daughters?" asked Estefan.

"He thought the creatures were dead. When he found his daughters, he made more and carries it with him. As long as we have it on, it will protect us. It is death to the creatures if it comes into contact with them."

"Let's get going," said Estefan, dismissing the story with a wave of a hand.

BLOCK FELT his stomach lurch when he saw Estefan and Brosnev carrying a body from the ruins.

"Son of a bitch." He felt ashamed for not believing the civilian's story. As soon as Estefan was close enough, he spoke. "Sergeant, tell me everything."

"There's one more body, sir."

"Have Brosnev and Lauki bring it and you brief me on what you saw."

While Brosnev and Lauki retrieved the second body, Estefan told Block what they saw at the scene. When the second body was in the vehicle, Block called for Brosnev.

"Tell Lauki I'm sorry for his loss," said Block. Brosnev immediately translated Block's condolences. Lauki's gaze never left the ruined buildings.

"Shock probably," offered Estefan.

"When we get back, make sure he gets to medical," said Block.

"Yes sir."

"Did you photograph the site?"

"No sir," Estefan replied. "I'll go back and do it now."

Block knew photographs would be required for the report. Any incident involving mysterious deaths was highly scrutinized. He had to examine the site personally so that his report would be accurate. The last thing he wanted to do was piss off the colonel again.

"Stay here. Keep an eye on Lauki. I don't like the way he looks. Where were the bodies?"

"Right by the first standing wall you come to. They were lying directly in front of it."

"I'll be right back." Block took a camera from his case and headed toward the ruins. Lauki reached for his bottle, but Block was gone before he could use it. He spoke with urgency to Brosnev, grasping the lapel on his jacket.

"He says we need to get the Captain out of here right now! He's quite adamant about it. He doesn't have the elixir to protect him and—"

"He's just going to take a look, and be right back, it should only be a few minutes. Tell him to calm down or I'll put the cuffs on him."

Estefan reached for the captain's pack of cigarettes lying on the seat, took one out, and lit it with his own lighter.

BLOCK HURRIED to the site. Murphy's Law once again reared its ugly head. *I can't screw this up. I'm not an incompetent fool like the colonel thinks. I'll do this one by the book and show him.*

He stopped in front of the wall and began photographing the surrounding area. There wasn't much natural light left so he used the flash. He was just about finished when he turned and saw a dark shape of someone standing not far from him.

"Who's there?"

No answer.

"I said who's there?"

No answer. He thought he perceived a shifting in the shadows. The one figure appeared to have been joined by another, maybe more. He let the camera hang by its strap around his neck as his hand moved to his holster.

"I have a weapon. Identify yourself."

The dark figures moved toward him. He took his weapon out of his holster.

"Stop! I have a weapon!" He didn't want to shoot. He had one murder investigation already, if he killed a national, scrutiny would fall heavily upon him. If he called out for Brosnev to translate, it might be interpreted the wrong way and provoke them.

Flipping the safety off, he fired a shot into the air.

"Stay where you are," he said. They stopped their approach. *Good. They know I mean business.* Then his hopes were dashed as he heard the laughter of the men as they moved toward him.

He started to backtrack as quick as he could without falling, but they surrounded him. Seeing no other alternative, he stopped and fired at them, emptying his magazine. They kept coming...then they were upon him. He saw their faces, the unholy glow of their eyes, and their fangs.

"Oh my God!" He screamed.

THE SOUND OF gunfire rang out from the ruins. Estefan drew his weapon. In the distance he could barely make out Captain Block running backwards toward them, firing his gun repeatedly at someone chasing him.

"What the shit!" said Estefan. Brosnev, his weapon drawn, also watched what was happening, and came to stand beside him.

"They can't be more then ten feet apart, point blank range. Whoever it is should be down hard!" Brosnev said. "Shouldn't we shoot?"

"No! They're too close together. Might hit the Captain. Look! The son of a bitch is still up and coming, gaining on him! The bullets have no effect!" Estefan added. "Look, there's two of them, no three...four altogether!"

They watched the mysterious attackers pounce on the captain. His screams lingered on the night air as they began to tear him limb from limb; the shreds of flesh and bone appearing like streamers in the early evening light.

Lauki took the bottle and handed it to Brosnev as he spoke. Brosnev handed it to Estefan and said, "He says to throw it at them! There is not enough to kill them, but it will slow them down long enough for us to get away!"

Estefan stared at the black-burgundy colored liquid in the bottle. His other hand clasped the butt of his gun. He'd seen the captain empty his magazine into them without any effect. He took a few steps away from the vehicle and hurled the bottle toward the attackers who now eyed them as the next target. The bottle struck the hard ground about five feet in front of them, causing a spray to splatter them. They recoiled with a screeching sound that Estefan had never heard before and would never forget for the rest of his life.

"Get in the vehicle—NOW!"

Everyone scrambled inside. Estefan jumped into the driver's seat and drove as fast as he could, much quicker than the roads allowed. They were tossed about the vehicle like rag dolls, Estefan constantly fighting to keep control of the vehicle from going off the road and into a ditch. The creatures did not pursue them, trapped by the mysterious liquid. He tried to erase the horrific images from his mind, but the sight of the captain being torn apart refused to subside from his thoughts.

BROSNEV WATCHED as Estefan drove the vehicle to Camp Bondsteel without saying a word even after attempts to communicate with him. Brosnev wondered if Estefan was in some kind of shock after seeing the captain killed. He hoped Estefan would be able to finish the trip to the base camp. Idriz Lauki sat silent in his seat, sporadically glancing at the bodies of his daughters and verifying that the creatures had not followed them.

The vehicle proceeded to the gate of Camp Bondsteel; the guard recognized Sergeant Estefan and waved them through. Estefan stopped the vehicle at the medical tent, just outside the main entrance door. He turned off the engine and became immobile, staring straight ahead.

Brosnev jumped out, shook him, and yelled at him. There was no response. He told Lauki to stay put and he went inside the tent for help. He returned with a doctor and an MP; they helped get Estefan out of the vehicle and into the examination room.

Taking a moment to rest, Brosnev realized that he was the senior soldier left to the ill-fated mission, and it was his duty to make a full report on what had happened as soon as possible. He located a telephone and called Colonel Antol. As he waited for the colonel to answer, he rehearsed in his mind how he was going to explain what had happened. When he heard the colonel's rough "yes." Brosnev stuttered through a brief explanation of events. The colonel ordered him not to say anything to anyone until he arrived.

Brosnev went back out to the vehicle where Lauki waited with the corpses of his daughters. Grief stricken, he stroked their hair and quietly spoke to the dead girls. Brosnev placed his hand on the man's shoulder, trying to offer comfort.

"When will the horrible beasts be killed?" Lauki asked in his native tongue.

"I don't know," Brosnev answered. "But something will be done. We have confirmed your story. I have seen them with my own eyes."

"These creatures are very old, they are very wise to the habits of mankind and they are not easy to kill. It will take...much. We have tormented each other through the generations. Even I have sought out revenge...and thought I had achieved it. But look where that has gotten me. My poor girls are dead. First their mother to the Serbs and now my babies to these creatures. But I will—"

Colonel Antol's jeep pulled up to the medical tent, interrupting the words of Lauki. The base commander jumped out. "Inside, now!" he ordered.

A moment later a truckload of MPs arrived and encircled the area.

The colonel emerged.

"Get those two bodies inside immediately," he barked to the medical personnel. "I want them autopsied at once. All personnel here are not to leave this area unless I personally approve it." The medical personnel stared at the Base Commander for a few seconds in disbelief, wondering what had happened to warrant such protocol.

"I said now, damn it!"

The personnel immediately did as they were ordered.

"Who is the duty medical officer?"

"I am sir." A young man stepped forward. "Major Barkley."

"What is the sergeant's condition?"

"He's stable, but appears to be in shock. He's unresponsive now, but he might come around with time. We have him under observation."

"No one talks to him unless I say so. Perform the autopsies at once. I need to know what killed the girls."

"Yes sir, I'll get started right away," he said and left.

Antol turned toward Brosnev and Lauki. "Corporal I want you to find a quiet room and write down everything that happened since you left here, and finish with the moment you called me," he said. "This is an incredible story. You're sure you are not stretching it somewhat?"

"No sir. What I explained to you was exactly what happened."

"We have a senior sergeant that is in shock, you say the Captain was murdered, and you bring two dead bodies back with you. I'd say that gives some credibility to your story. In fact, there is significant interest from stateside in this matter, and when they hear about this development, God only knows what will happen next."

"Sir, what about the civilian?"

"He has to stay here. He'll need to answer a lot of questions as the investigation intensifies. Take him with you and have him write down his version. We'll have someone else translate it later."

Brosnev spoke to Lauki, telling him what they were going to do. Lauki nodded his head accompanied by words and then a half-hearted laugh.

"What did he say?" Antol asked.

"He says he has no where else to go. The creatures want him dead."

Brosnev and Lauki started walking away to find a place to write their statements.

"Corporal," Antol called.

Brosnev stopped and looked back at the Base Commander. "Yes sir?"

"Did Captain Block...did he suffer?"

"Horribly sir." Brosnev turned away and tried not to imagine the scene of the captain's death.

CHAPTER 2

"DID YOU READ this?" General Stone asked Commander Scott as he
showed him a folder labeled "Camp Bondsteel Situation Report." Scott
saw the folder's title and felt his stomach sink and his body
temperature rise by about ten degrees. He'd been afraid of this. He
knew the general would react strongly to it. The file contained a report
from the base commander of Camp Bondsteel, part of the multinational
peace effort in Kosovo, and detailed a rather unusual occurrence
regarding a story about the mysterious deaths of two civilians. Scott
had removed it from the general's reading pile because he knew if he
read it, all hell would probably break loose. Seeing the report in
Stone's hand, he found himself wishing he'd never seen the damned
thing and that he didn't work for this madman.

General Stone, the Commander of U.S. Special Operations
Command (SOCOM) at MacDill Air Force Base in Florida, looked like
someone who had found the cure for cancer. He was a large man, in
excellent shape for a man of fifty plus years. His close- cropped gray
hair was characteristic of a career soldier, the high and tight. He was
always immaculate in uniform; it gave him an air of arrogance. His
face, brown eyes, high cheekbones, and square jaw, never gave away
information about his position on issues. He controlled all the Special
Forces of the military services, and certain projects kept at the highest
secrecy levels. He was a man of great power and influence.

His aspirations were high and remained that way and he used his
prowess for solving impossible problems as his stepladder to those
aspirations. He had been accused on occasion for being too Patton-like
in his actions; at times exceeding his authority by committing to acts
not sanctioned by higher-ups. Still, his record was impressive, his
accomplishments long, and his retirement far away. His outlook was
that there was a need for a man of his forward thinking in an age of
softies. Politicians who had never served in the military, had taken over
too many of the roles that controlled the military forces.

One of his biggest complaints was the lack of commitment of
military assets to the drug war. Although illegal drugs was a world

problem, this particular area hit closest to him; he'd lost his sixteen-year-old son, his only child, to an overdose of cocaine. His wife blamed him and his career that kept him away from home for long periods of time, but he saw the greater problem: Businessmen with political connections who controlled large portions of the illicit drug trade and reaped it's blood-money profits.

Scott distinctly remembered the dissertation the general had given him on the subject, about how the administration only threw token money and effort against the drug problem. Nobody wanted to step too hard on the toes of the country's South American neighbors. Everyone knew the only way to succeed on the war on drugs was to pull the plug on the Colombian cartels, take them out, take them all out by any means possible.

Although the general had many subordinates who looked through the multitude of media that flowed through the information center on a daily basis, he still made it a point to scan through some of it himself. Most of the reports were for information purposes only, such as this report. But Stone had made it known that he wanted to see anything that sounded the least bit strange. The more bizarre the information or story, the better. Nothing was dismissed, no matter how weird. To not adhere to this order might invoke the general's wrath, which had been known to end many a career.

Stone had the mind of a steel trap. It contained reams of information that the casual person would dismiss as unusable or uninformative. He stored everything away and had a phenomenal recall he called his "problem-solving store." Whenever he needed answers, he just went shopping through the warehouse of information, putting bits of pieces together and coming out with solutions.

Lately though, with all that was going on in the Balkan region, first Bosnia and Herzegovina and now Kosovo, his thoughts remained focused on these areas. He found the history of the region fascinating because of the campaigns that changed the political and military landscape of this region over the past several thousand years, along with the interesting topics about the myths and legends of the Balkans.

Commander Scott stared at the report that General Stone had in his upraised hand. Scott recalled it had been filed by a young Army Captain who had been the duty officer when the incident occurred. The report concluded that the deaths of the girls and Captain Block was possibly the result of Serbians, but Scott knew that the unusual comments from the civilian who had reported the incident had kindled the general's interest. The words "vampires" and "creatures" keyed his attention although the base commander had dismissed the use of the terms to translation problems and possible hysteria brought on by war fatigue.

"Yes sir, I have seen it," Scott replied, trying to keep his voice even. His heart beat rapidly as the general's gaze bore through him. Sweat began to ooze from his pores.

"And?"

"Hysteria and war fatigue," he responded, his mouth becoming very dry.

"So you think someone is fabricating all of this?"

"Yes sir," he answered. "Those people have been through a lot. Hysteria from deaths of loved ones can lead to fabrication of stories as a kind of repression of guilt. We've seen this before in Bosnia."

"Very rational thinking commander," Stone said as he closed the folder. Scott breathed a sigh of relief, thinking that the storm had passed. He returned to the work on his desk.

"But I disagree, commander," Stone's voice boomed back causing him to jump in his seat. "I think there are some interesting facts here that need to be looked at."

"But sir..." Scott began. "There can't possible be any truth—"

"Listen to me." Stone cut him off. "I want you to do the following."

Scott scrambled to get a pen and paper.

"One, send a communication to the base commander telling him to check out the story. Two, put the Special Forces unit in the area on alert and three, get me someone with a background in historical, cultural, myths, and legends of this area."

"Does that include vampires, sir?" Scott asked and wished he could retract the question. A bead of sweat scurried down his back.

"It does, commander," Stone said and smiled as he stepped up to within a few inches of his face. "And if you keep something like this from me again, I'll put you in the biggest shit-hole I can find, do you understand?"

"Yes...yes sir, I understand." Stone stared at him for seconds, but Scott thought it was much longer. Finally, the general left his office. He exhaled strongly and wished he'd never taken this assignment. He pitied whomever was assigned to this mission.

NAVY COMMANDER John Reese, called Reese by those who knew him, was right at an intriguing point in the book he was reading when the phone rang. He thought about ignoring it, but the interruption had destroyed his concentration. He tried to organize the mass of paper that surrounded him so it wouldn't get it mixed up when he got up. The papers were his notes that would comprise his book he'd been working on for a few years. Titled *Myths and Legends*, he hoped it would become a textbook for classes of the same subject.

Many of the classes he'd taken while earning a masters degree in Ancient Civilizations and Mythology did not have good textbooks; reliable information was scarce. His textbook would go further than any book currently published by basing the entire premise on the effect of legends and myths in the current day environment. As soon as he could afford the time and the cost, he planned a research trip to Europe to gather hard data. His deepest hope and desire was to prove just one of his theories correct.

He finally reached the ringing phone. "Hello," he said, unable to keep the aggravation out of his voice.

"Commander Reese?"

"Yes." The use of his military rank indicated this was a formal call.

"This is Captain Bleth. I'm the duty officer for Commander Mid-Atlantic Region in Norfolk."

"Yes sir, how can I help you?" Reese asked, civilizing his tone as he was speaking with a senior officer.

"We've received immediate orders for you from Washington. You are to proceed immediately to U.S. Special Operations Command at MacDill Air Force Base in Florida."

"What?" Reese knew they must have the wrong guy. "There must be some mistake. I'm the logistics officer for Naval Special Warfare Group Two at Little Creek. Sir, are you sure you're not looking for another Commander Reese?"

"Is your social security number 198-65-8465?"

"Yes sir."

"There is no mistake," said the captain.

"I'll have to notify my chain of command."

"Your chain of command has been notified about your departure. The orders are not permanent change of station, just temporary assignment for an undetermined time."

After twenty years of service, he thought that there would be no shock when unexpected notification came, but there always was, as was the quick acceptance that followed. "When do I depart?"

"There is a flight out of Norfolk Air Station in three hours, you are to be on that plane."

"Is there any explanation of the assignment?" He looked at his watch. It would only take him thirty minutes to be on the Naval Air Station from his home in Ocean View.

"All it says is temporary assignment to an advisory position of some type. I'll have a duty driver meet you at the air terminal with copies of your orders."

"Thank you sir," Reese said. His mind raced with the possibilities.

"Have a good time."

Reese was slow in returning the phone to the cradle. He sat in his chair and organized his thoughts. It was quite strange that there had been no prior warning that new orders were coming. Not even a call from his immediate superior in his change of command, Captain Clark.

He opened his recall folder and looked for the telephone number for Clark. This assignment to the Special Warfare Group had introduced him to some new and interesting operations that were different than the regular Navy side of the house, but they did not compare to the strange orders he'd just received. He was in charge of the group for purchasing supplies and services required for use by the Special Operation Units on the East Coast. His work dealt mainly with the SEAL units and similar forces that introduced him to darker side of Naval Operations. After a year, he had developed a unique respect for the elite of the Special Warfare Community.

He found the number and dialed it.

"Hello."

"Captain Clark?"

"Reese?"

"Yes sir. I'm sorry to bother you at home but—"

"The duty officer called you already?"

"Yes sir. Did they explain to you what this is all about?"

"Afraid not. I tried to call you a few minutes ago to give you a heads up. Your line was busy. All I know is that I got a call from Captain Sorbert, Commander Naval Special Warfare Group Two, telling me not to look for you on Monday morning. When I asked him why, I was told to not worry about it, that you would be on special assignment to SOCOM for an undetermined period of time. I pressed him for more information but he was closed-mouth about it. Sorry, Reese."

"Do you have any idea what this might mean?"

"I hate to speculate, but usually when orders are cut this fast, it's done high up in the chain of command. Whoever wants you there, has to have a lot of pull to do this. Must be important."

"But it doesn't make any sense sir."

"Maybe not to you, but it obviously does to someone else. All you can do is go along for now and when you get there, you'll find out for sure."

"Thanks for your time, Captain Clark."

"Have a good trip. Give me a call if you can and be careful."

"Thank you sir." Reese hung up the phone.

What was this about? He had to admit that his interest was now peaked as to why he'd been chosen. He mentally ticked off his qualifications: degrees in economics for his business side and ancient history for his personal interest. He was a logistics officer with a diverse background but nothing spectacular that would guarantee promotion, which was why he'd retire in another eighteen months. He possessed a top-secret clearance that was required for the current assignment and his current superior respected him. This led him to believe that it had to be something to do with logistics in the Special Operations community. Maybe some research and development contractual issues or something had come up on some project and they were looking for some fresh thoughts.

That's probably it, nothing too exciting, it was just the community way to issue orders and move personnel around unexpectedly, keeps us on our toes. He looked at the clock and decided he better get moving and pack some clothes even though he was not even sure how long he would be staying in Florida.

He made it on time to the airport and was met by the duty driver. What surprised him, no, what shocked him was that the plane was for him, and only him; a small passenger plane normally reserved for VIPs. Extremely odd that a plane that cost serious bucks to operate would ferry him to Florida whereas normal procedure would have placed him on a contracted passenger plane. Whatever awaited him in Florida was urgent enough to warrant the expenditure.

Greeted by one of the pilots, a lieutenant, he was seated only seconds before the plane rolled down the runway. He took a book from his brief case titled *Creatures in Our Lives*, opened it to the page he had tabbed, and began reading.

"Excuse me sir, but a book with a title like that must be strange."

Reese looked up and saw another lieutenant. By the insignia on his uniform, he was also a pilot.

"Yea, it is kind of strange." He offered his hand. "John Reese."

"Lieutenant Sam Kramer, I'm the co-pilot."

"You wouldn't have any idea why I'm being flown to MacDill, would you?"

"No sir, they just hand us the paper that says who and when."

"I guess I'll have to wait until I get there then."

"So what's the book about?"

"A lot of different things dealing with folklore and myth."

"Really? I had this professor once...I was taking a theology course in college. You know, one of those have-to-take courses. Anyway, he went off on some tangent about folklore and stuff like that," said Kramer.

"There is a school of thought that to study something based upon myth, legends or folklore, it was considered similar to the study of theology. There is no hardcore evidence that could either prove or disprove the stories. Therefore it became a study of philosophy, whereby one's faith or belief was the deciding factor. On a more personal level if it was evident that the individual lacked the courage or determination to become involved in an area that could solidly be disproved such as hard science, it was likely to be determined that the person was a slacker one way or another."

"Interesting comparison, it's a...unique area to get into. How did you get interested in something like that?"

"I think I developed this passion for monsters at an early age after seeing the early Dracula and werewolf movies. I was astounded to learn that these creatures were based upon myths that had been documented in some form. My interest grew from there, although when I attended college, I studied in the business field out of practicality, leaving my passion for the unknown and unexplained as a hobby."

"It's a shame how we ignore our true passion while we do things just to earn a buck. The whole concept sounds fascinating. I bet you have wooed many a lady with your stories of these creatures."

Reese grinned. "Most women who learned about my favorite pastime assumed I was an immature jerk. I have to admit I spend a lot of time consumed in research. Women tend to maintain their distance—guess that's why I'm still single."

"Personally, commander, I don't think there is a whole lot of difference between strange creatures and wives. Take it from someone with experience; I'm on number three."

"Can I quote you on that?" Reese asked.

"Hell no, sir. I can't afford another ex."

Both men laughed.

"I better get back to the flight deck," said Kramer. "Nice talking to you, commander."

"Same here. Hope I didn't ramble on too much."

"No sir. Sit back and enjoy the flight."

MACDILL AIR Force Base was located about eight miles south of Tampa, Florida, on the tip of the Interbay Peninsula in Hillsborough County. As the plane taxied to the receiving end of the runway, Reese noticed a car waiting there. If someone sent a special plane to retrieve him, then the car was probably there to pick him up. The duty driver, a Marine Corporal, saluted him and said that he was to take him to headquarters.

They arrived at a two-story building and the corporal indicated that he was to enter the center doors. Reese thanked him and headed into the building. The reception area was plain and carried the usual adornments of most military installations. On the walls was the colorful depiction of the individual service logos that fell together under one umbrella of command, the Navy SEALs, the Army Airborne, and the Air Force Special Operations Forces, all circling a larger emblem of the Unites States Special Operation Command. The main centerpiece was the tip of a lance, sometimes referred to as the ace of spades.

"Can I help you sir?" asked the young soldier sitting at the reception desk.

"Yes," Reese said as he handed his orders to the soldier. He immediately placed a call.

"Someone will be right here."

"Thanks."

He occupied his time by looking at the standard chain of command picture board that resided on every military command. Within a few minutes, a Navy Commander appeared.

"John Reese," he said as he extended his hand. "I'm Sam Scott."

"Pleased to meet you." Reese refrained from asking him what was going on. He observed that Scott was not a logistics officer. He was a line officer. He recognized the two rank insignia on his collars versus the one that he had. Staff corps officers wore one rank; the other collar depicted specialty.

Scott was tall and thin and looked like someone who had been run ragged most of his time in the service. Reese knew the signs of a person trying to achieve promotion and position at an accelerated pace, right down to the darkness under his eyes and a slight nervousness.

"I know you have questions," said Scott, "and I apologize for the short notice. If you follow me, we can go somewhere where we can talk."

"Sounds good." Reese followed. Scott used a magnetic card to access the doors they went through. Reese was surprised at the maze orientation of the facility and imagined he'd get lost in here without someone escorting him.

As they proceeded, Reese noticed that the doors took on a new look; the verbiage on signs became more authoritative. He noticed that not only was the card required, but also there were Marine guards who verified Scott and his credentials.

After a few minutes, they entered a small windowless conference room that contained one large circular table with eight chairs around it. Scott gestured for him to have a seat.

"Coffee?" asked Scott.

"Sure." Reese sat in a chair. He was anxious to hear about his new assignment.

Scott placed a cup of coffee in front of him, then sat.

"Why am I here?" Reese asked. "Why the rush?"

Scott exhaled. "You have a background that may be of use to us."

"My logistics. That what I thought," John said, relieved. "You want me to work in the acquisition and logistics center?"

"No, it's your other non-Navy interest—ancient histories and civilizations. Your interest in myths and legends."

"What? You have to be kidding right? I don't understand what that has to do with...the Navy or the military for that matter. It's more like a hobby for me."

"It does have relevance in this particular case, or at least we believe it does. We have come across some...well...before I explain any of that you must understand about General Stone. He is an extraordinary leader and tactician. He is known for his unusual approaches in solving the unsolvable, he's almost a legend." Reese was surprised at Scott's tone. It was almost as if he was apologizing for the general. How odd.

"I have heard of him and his accomplishments," said Reese. General Stone was well known throughout the services.

"Good. He likes to look into the unusual or bizarre events we sometimes come across. Most of them don't pan out and can be explained by rational means, but every once in a while something unexplainable is found."

"Interesting approach, but I still don't see where I come in," Reese said. He sipped his coffee.

"Your background appears to be extensive in the European

Theater and the Balkans."

"Yes, many scholars consider those areas the center of many myth creations, so my interests lie there as well."

"With all the happenings in Kosovo," Scott said, "there have been some unusual developments. The general felt that someone with your background might be useful on his staff."

"That's it?" John asked, amazed at the simplicity of it. "You flew me out here on a private jet—with a few hours notice—to be an advisor on what I do for a hobby?"

"That's it."

"Then why all the mystery, the cloak-and-dagger orders and stuff?"

"Politics. The general doesn't like others to know that he is looking into any different areas. Rumors can ruin a career faster than anything else in the military."

"True," Reese said. "A good many personnel have been forced—"

The door opened and General Stone entered like a thoroughbred racehorse that had just shot through the opening gate in a race. Reese almost knocked over his cup of coffee as he stood to greet the general.

"As you were," said the general not even sounding the least bit winded from his entry. "You must be Commander Reese," he said as he extended out his hand. Reese took the hand and shook it, noticing that in the general's other hand he had a folder marked TOP SECRET.

"Yes sir, pleased to meet you," Reese said, feeling a little apprehensive.

"Thought you might find this interesting reading on the flight," said the general as he handed the folder to Reese.

"Flight...sir?" Reese asked. He assumed he would have a desk job.

"Your flight to Kosovo leaves within the hour. There is something there that I want you to see."

AS THE PLANE departed MacDill AFB, Commander John Reese sat in awe at the way he was being shuffled around the globe. Seven hours ago he had been comfortably at home reading a book, then a mere hour ago, he had been in a conference room with Commander Scott and General Stone. Now he was on another plane heading to Kosovo, which was in the midst of civil unrest being control by NATO peacekeepers. Commander Scott had briefed him that the plane was bound for Skopie, Macedonia via Rota, Spain. He would be driven to

Camp Bondsteel in Kosóvo. Specific information about his assignment was in the folder that the general had given him, and everything else would become clear upon his arrival at the base camp.

The only difference from his earlier flight was that he was not alone on this plane; he had lots of company. This was a regular run. Personnel from all branches of the services filled most seats. Their conversations were excited and busied as new acquaintances were made and stories exchanged. Reese had been assigned a seat by himself, the flight captain told him he would understand when he read the information he had been given.

Reese still had a hard time wondering why his knowledge of ancient history and folklore would be of use to the Navy. What would warrant this? It puzzled him. The more he thought about it, the better it looked. He had always wanted to go to this particular region to study and to look for information. He held the folder that General Stone had given him, still unopened due to the haste that was required to board the plane prior to departure.

As the plane settled into a cruising altitude, he opened the folder. Immediately on top of the contents page, there was a warning that the information was classified and that by the flight conclusion, the plane commander had orders to destroy the folder and contents before touching down on foreign soil. He felt his stomach lurch. What the hell did this file contain?

He read initial reports from the Camp Bondsteel Base Commander about one incident with an encounter with a civilian named Idriz Lauki and his story about his daughters' deaths. Histories from that part of ancient Europe were filled with similar claims about deaths caused by creatures. The majority of these stories had been attributed to imagination and exceptional tale-wielding by local inhabitants, but a few defied logic and reasoning and left room for speculation.

Next, was an order issued to the Base Commander, Colonel Antol, by General Stone, its verbiage couched as another possible ethnic cleansing incident that required immediate follow-up. Another report followed, filed twenty-fours hours ago from the Base Commander claiming that a Captain Block sent to investigate the incident was now missing and possibly murdered by party or parties unknown at the site of the previous murders. The murders of two girls were confirmed by the retrieval of two bodies from the site.

The Captain failed to return from the site, Sergeant Estefan was under medical custody and appeared to be in shock from what he had witnessed. The other soldier, Corporal Brosnev, and the civilian, Idriz Lauki, submitted statements but their comments had not been verified with another on-site visit pending the request from SOCOM to not take action until their specialist arrived. Reese was now categorized by his new orders as the specialist.

Reese flipped to those reports and read what sounded like something directly out of a horror movie. They were like many accounts he had read through his studies, but this time there seemed to be an additional credibility by the military being involved. There would be no point for military personnel to lie about such events. Still, it could be just a cover-up to confuse the ethnic cleansing issue. If another party could be blamed in having taken part in the killing, it could benefit the Serbians.

He flipped to the medical reports on the autopsies of the two civilian casualties. Reese didn't understand most of the annotations on the standard Department of Defense form. He turned it over and focused on a general comment block at the bottom. He read the comments once, twice, then put down the report and stared out the window. Under cause of death, the words "loss of all blood" were underlined followed by, "no blood or traces of blood left in body, as if drained."

Reese tasted bile from his soured stomach. He willed his stomach under his control. Here was exactly what he hoped to find, verified on paper, the classic signs of a vampire attack. He had wondered if he'd encounter a creature from the myths and legends he had pored over. And now it was staring him right his face, but he calmed himself. The odds were against the story being true, a perpetrated hoax by the locals to scare people from the region. But there was a chance. "But why the interest from General Stone?" He muttered.

One page remained in the folder. The last page was a personal note from General Stone, "Commander Reese, you know what these mysterious factors may indicate. I want you to find out if there is any truth to what's been reported. All of SOCOM assets in the theater of operations are available at your disposal. Do not to talk to anyone about this except those that are cleared by Commander Scott or myself. Report only to me or to Commander Scott."

Reese's gaze settled on the last paragraph.

"Although the probability of this report being true is small, for a moment consider the possibility that it is a fact. Your personal interests lie in this area; mine for the use of such creatures as military assets. We can satisfy both our needs if we proceed carefully but quickly—if these claims turn out to be real."

Reese closed the folder and looked out of the window. He couldn't decide if he should feel excited about such a prospect, or if he should be scared.

He chose scared.

CHAPTER 3

1915

DIMITRI BICANNOFF sat next to the fire and listened to the runner's story. Mikel had come from the main Serbian force at the border. He was relaying the account of the battles between the invading Germans and the Serbian army, in between taking bites of stale bread and washing it down with cold water flavored with whiskey.

"They are advancing quickly across the border. We had achieved a stalemate between our army and Austria-Hungary national forces. Things weren't going well but at least we were holding them. But now the German bastards! They bring their Panzer tanks and armored forces. We are no match for them on the open battleground."

As the downfall of his country was foretold, Dimitri and his four friends, Josip, Franjo, Andre, and Iliga listened with interest in the frigid air. They were all in their mid- twenties and full of patriotic pride and spirit. All had lived in their village on the outskirts of Kacianik since they were born, farming the lands with their families, or what remained of them after the constant wars. All but Josip had lost their fathers in the Balkan wars of 1912 and 1913, leaving them with a greater role in supporting their families and that tied them to this little town.

Most families had five to eight children who were destined to die on the battlefield or in the fields from toiling from sunrise to sunset. The women, bound to the endless tasks of trying to keep their men alive as long as possible, were kept busy too. The worsening economy, the harsh conditions of farming, and the ceaseless battles for independence of the small but proud country stole their men.

Dimitri looked like his father, with hawk-like features. His face was weathered with lines of hard work and too many hours in a field behind the plow. Shaped by a difficult life, he looked like a man ten years older. He was large, slightly more than six feet and broad at the shoulders. His hair was jet black, peppered with gray. His demeanor encouraged his friends to follow him.

The rest of his friends looked similar with dark hair and brown eyes. All possessed varying degrees of haggard appearances. They knew they were destined for short lives. But now, they stood around the fire, their clothes stitched and mended to the point of non-recognition of what they must have looked like when they had been first made, listening to a story that had probably been told hundreds of times over the span of centuries in this country. But the story took them away from their toils in the field for a little while and they were riveted by it.

The cold seemed to no longer affect the young men as they listened to the man speak of the battles and fighting. The five of them were enthralled by the stories of how the Serbs fought bravely against the tanks of the Nazis, throwing themselves at the mountains of steel in attempts to slow them down or, if they were lucky enough, to destroy them.

"But now," Mikel continued, "our leaders think it wise to retreat and regroup at Corfu so that we can better organize for an offensive that would remove the German invaders from our homeland. Death to them all!"

The men stared at each other, their chests swelling with anticipation and pride for their country's soldiers.

"Death to them all!" Mikel repeated.

Dimitri stepped closer to the soldier, offering him more food and drink. The other four arranged the dwindling fire and fueled it with sparse sticks, their thoughts turning to the soldiers. Most of these soldiers had been farmers until they received the call to defend their homeland. Off the men had gone, many from this very village, while Dimitri and his friends had stayed and farmed the lands. Food was required to support the great army.

Their group was unique. Andre and Iliga were quiet men who needed someone to follow. Franjo was the reckless one of the bunch; always taking risks or dares. They all had bonded with Dimitri and Josip, who were closer than the others due to an incident as teenagers that had made them the best of friends.

"Death to them all!" Franjo said.

As the others waited for Mikel to tell them more, Dimitri's thoughts drifted to the day when he and Josip faced certain death.

"THE COW IS dead," the town elder said to the small crowd that had assembled at his home. "Mauled by a bear."

The crowd consisted of women, children, and old men who

murmured their fear and hatred of the beast and what the loss of food would mean this winter if more cattle were killed.

"We will have to wait until some of the men return to kill it. In the meantime, keep all your livestock nearby."

When the crowd left, Dimitri stood with Josip.

"We have to help the village," he said.

"This is a mean and vile creature," Josip began. "You heard what the elder said. We should wait."

"We don't know when our fathers will return from fighting. If we wait, more cattle may be killed."

"You know where the bear is?" asked Josip.

"I think so. Will you help me?"

Josip looked toward the elder's house, then at Dimitri. "Of course."

"Can you get your father's gun?"

"Yes."

"Good. I will bring my father's gun, too. Meet me outside of the ravine to the south of the village."

Before long, they stood at the entrance to the ravine, the sides opening into a large mouth but then disappearing into the darkness of the forests.

"We shall each take a side and meet at the other end in two hours," Dimitri said.

"The elder warns about getting separated in these woods along the ravine. He says they are very treacherous and—"

"You see the tip of that peak?" Dimitri said as he pointed north. "Keep it in view at all times. It will allow you to keep your progress in the right direction."

Dimitri waited for Josip to say something. He sensed the hesitation within his friend.

"We have scouted here before, why do you hesitate?"

"Hesitate? I do not hesitate. You are the one doing all the talking."

Dimitri slapped him on the back and smiled. Josip returned the gesture.

"We will be fine. If you see the bear, fire a shot, and I'll do the same. Meet you at the end."

Three hours later, Dimitri was waiting for Josip at their appointed meeting place. His failure to show had Dimitri worried. But no shot had been fired. Where could he be?

He started to walk in the direction that Josip would have taken.

After almost an hour of walking, the chaotic cackling of frightened birds off to his right startled him. Something had caused them to leave in a hurry.

He moved in that direction noticing the change of landscape as the rock walls grew taller and thicker, surely leading to a dead end. In his earlier explorations, he discovered there was only one way that led out, and this was not it. It would be the perfect spot for a hunter to lead its prey and then trap it. His fear that Josip may have been lured into the area quickened his pace.

His suspicions were confirmed as he heard the sounds of the bear snarling in anger. "Bastard!" he cried.

Moving as quietly as he could in order to preserve the element of surprise, Dimitri moved further inward until he could see the beast and Josip. Josip was perched precariously on a thin ledge. From what Dimitri could see, it was taking Josip every bit of strength and balance to maintain his position. This also explained why he had not fired the gun. If he tried to get it off of his shoulder, he might lose his grip and plummet. The huge bear was standing on its hind legs and swinging its razor sharp claws within inches of Josip's feet.

Dimitri removed his father's gun from his shoulder; its discolored stock and rusted gun barrel gave him a disquieted moment. What if it didn't fire this time? He had fired the gun before with his father at targets; it had worked most of the time.

He aimed squarely at the back of the bear, if he could hit the beast in the heart, a second shot wouldn't be necessary. Taking a deep breath and holding it, he fired.

Josip, exhausted from keeping his awkward position, was on the verge of falling off the ledge as Dimitri's shot struck the bear in the shoulder, clearly missing its heart. The crazed animal turned toward Dimitri.

Dimitri ejected the round and loaded another. As he threw the bolt forward, it got stuck halfway.

"Damn! It's jammed," he said as fear slammed into him, numbing his body. He tried to turn to run, but couldn't move. Everything around him slowed down to a horrific crawl. He became aware of his own breathing and the beating of his heart. With a surprising but calm matter of fact manner, he knew his life would soon be over.

Looking toward the bear, he saw it was watching him curiously. As a wind blew by Dimitri the bear raised its head and sniffed. As if the beast could smell his fear, it uttered an ear-shattering growl, lowered its head and charged.

Dimitri shut his eyes.

Josip fell to the ground and even though badly cramped from his holding position of the ledge, un-shouldered his rifle and fired as the bear surged toward Dimitri. If he missed, his friend would die, and he might too.

The bear fell within inches of Dimitri's feet.

Dimitri opened his eyes and looked at the dead animal. He watched as its blood began to soak the ground around it and finally realized that the creature was dead. Dimitri staggered to Josip and collapsed next to him. They sat silently and stared at the eight hundred-pound carcass. They hugged each other as their feelings of having escaped death surfaced.

"We have looked at death," Dimitri uttered.

"Yes," Josip replied.

"I've never realized how precious life is to me until faced with death. That moment when I thought I would die, I would have given anything to continue to live. Anything for another chance—"

"THANK YOU, I have had enough to eat," Mikel said, the sound of his voice bringing Dimitri out of his thoughts of the past, back to the cold night and the tales of the war.

"Our army will be coming through Montenegro and over the Albanian Mountains, " said Mikel. "It will be a long march and the winter is descending upon us. The terrain will slow down the German tanks, but we need to slow down the invaders on foot. Our plan calls for small teams of soldiers left at critical points who will hamper the onward onslaught of the attackers, buying precious time for the main force to get to Corfu. One of these points is a pass through the mountain not far from this village. It is my responsibility to arrange volunteers to man it before I rejoin the main force."

Dimitri's eyes lit up at the words; he looked for a similar reaction from his four friends.

"Do you know of any volunteers?" asked Mikel.

Dimitri looked at his friends and they agreed without a word between them. Dimitri would speak for the group; he'd always done so in the past.

"We will do it," said Dimitri. "It will be our honor to serve our great country to rid the bastard Germans from our soil. We will do it as our grandfathers rid the Turks from our land and as our fathers defeated the invaders from Bulgaria." The words made him feel proud as courage flowed through his veins. Their chance to fight for their country had finally arrived.

"Good," Mikel said, but not with enthusiasm, as he lowered his eyes from the young Dimitri knowing that he had just sentenced these young men to die against the hardened and experienced forces that were invading.

"Get your things together, we will leave at first light."

DIMITRI AND his group had much to do that night to make preparations to depart in the morning. There was no discussion amongst their group of who would be in charge. Dimitri, being the oldest had always been the leader, but more so because they believed in him. He visited and assured all of their families that it was only a temporary assignment and that they would return once they were sure that the advance of the Germans had been halted. Dimitri's mother said very little, only that when her husband had been called to the Balkan War that it, too, was only a temporary assignment from which he never returned.

His last visit was to Josip's home.

"Wait here," Josip said.

"Do you not want me to talk with your father?"

"I will talk to him—alone."

Dimitri saw the sullen look on Josip's face. "Are you sure?"

"Yes. My father will always be ashamed that he refused to go off to the Balkan War. All the others from the village had been killed. He knows that I have paid the price for his decision."

"But this is your chance to redeem your family's honor."

"I know. But..."

"But what?"

"You remember the time with the bear?"

"Of course."

"When I told my father about it, he said I was spared death because it would have been an honest death."

"Honest death?"

"Yes. He believes that I am destined to die a horrible death without honor because of what he has done. Superstition and the old ways—it is all he believes."

"Nonsense."

"Maybe. But I will talk to him alone because he will go on about it again. There's no point in you having to listen to his ranting."

"As you wish," Dimitri said placing his hand on Josip's shoulder.

"I will see you in the morning."

Dimitri returned home thinking about what Josip had told him. As he slipped into bed, he wondered what Josip's father thought about his life being spared. Did he survive in order to die another way also? But he had done nothing wrong. His father had gone off to the war.

"Foolish old man." Dimitri closed his eyes and went to sleep.

The following morning, their feet crunching on the frozen ground, the five young men and Mikel headed for the pass in the mountains near the village.

"Where exactly are we going?" asked Dimitri.

"It's called different things by people. You call it Devil's Grip. I call it the Pass of Death because of the battle in the late 1300s with the Turks. A legion of their soldiers were ambushed by the Serbians and massacred in the pass with no escape."

"Such a sad place," said Iliga.

"Well, yes and no." Mikel said. "You see, after the battle, a small group of monks established a monastery in the region, they wanted to—how do you say? Purify the place. They wanted to cleanse the evil by doing something good. They wanted their monastery to be special. It became the main resource for literature and history books that still remained in print."

"Books?" asked Franjo.

"Yes. Since the time of its establishment, they had amassed thousands of volumes of various subjects. People would come from all over to read and study the texts they preserved."

"What happened to it?" asked Iliga.

"The library remained for three hundred years until its destruction by a mysterious fire. All of the monks were killed as they attempted to save their books that were supposedly stored in deep caverns underneath the monastery. Burned to the ground. The ruins are still visible."

"You know what they else say about that place?" said Josip. "My grandmother told me that the monks weren't really monks at all but devil worshippers. They also did sacrifices...blood sacrifices to the devil."

"Old wives tales," Dimitri said with a casual air of dismissal. "I, too, have heard the stories of this place from my father. They are bedtime tales."

"I've heard some say that the monks that were killed there haunt it—still trying to save their books," continued Josip.

The soldier chuckled and waved his arm. "All grandmothers have stories to tell, don't they? The werewolves that stole the newborns was my grandmother's favorite."

They all chuckled at Mikel's comment, knowing that it was true. The country was full of ruins and cemeteries that left no wanting for any story that could possibly be imagined. "Don't worry," said Mikel. "You won't be that close to the ruins. There are some caves I saw on my way through that will offer shelter to you as you keep guard. You won't have to stay at the ruins."

The group breathed sighs of relief.

"How long do you think it will be before the Germans come?" asked Dimitri.

"Maybe a week, maybe a month, and maybe not at all," answered Mikel with a shrug. "Damn Germans are crazy. Only God knows what they will do."

They arrived late in the afternoon and made camp at one of the caves that Mikel had seen on his previous trip.

"There is plenty of room here for all of you. With some work, the cave could be shaped into habitable living quarters, and easily protect you from attack," said Mikel.

They built a fire that was hidden from sight by anyone approaching the pass and settled in for the night.

"The first thing we must do tomorrow is establish lookouts and plan a trap in case the Germans come through—along with your plan of escape. I have explosives and weapons that I will leave with you, but I must make sure you know how to use them."

"We will kill them with our bare hands if we must," Dimitri said causing a rowdy stir from his friends. As their leader, he knew he must keep their spirits up. For now, talk would be the tool he chose.

Mikel smiled sadly. "I thought that way once. Have you ever killed anyone before?" He looked at each young man's face, but he could already tell that they had not. "It is easier to kill at a distance than it is to kill up close. If you do it up close you may either lose your nerve and be killed, or you may kill and be damned by nightmares the rest of your lives. Either way, you're damned if you have any kind of conscience at all. Yes, you'll be haunted for the rest of your lives." Mikel ignored their disbelieving expressions and lay down to sleep.

Dimitri looked at Mikel and wondered about the foreboding he felt that had accompanied the soldier's words of death and of killing. He wondered if Mikel could see inside of him and know he was scared and know the doubts he had about risking his life. He saw the other men looking at him and knew he needed to say something to reassure them.

"It's the whiskey talking," Dimitri said softly. "It makes his words awkward and unworthy for a soldier of the great army of Serbia."

"We have seen death before. Those that died in the village from old age that came too early in their lives," replied Josip.

"But we have not killed another human before. Only sick farm animals or the wolves or bears that prey on our cattle during the winter months," added Andre.

"I can do it," Dimitri said, trying to bolster his own confidence. Inside he wondered if he really would be able to kill when the time came. *But I must put aside my doubts if I am to be responsible for the lives of my friends.*

"If Dimitri can, so can I," said Josip.

"And I!" echoed the remaining three friends.

"We have all been raised in religious homes, but the killing of those that seek to remove our freedom will be forgiven. For our country," said Dimitri as he raised his metal cup to initiate the toast and dispel their fears, especially his own.

"For our country," the rest agreed. They raised their glasses and drank.

Dimitri hoped there would be no more thoughts about killing, thanks to the whiskey. They drank some more, then drifted off to sleep.

THE GERMAN patrol watched the six men as they slept around the diminishing campfire.

"They are nothing," the seasoned sergeant said to the lieutenant. "Just farmers, maybe one excuse of a soldier amongst them. We should not waste time—"

"It doesn't matter. Our orders are clear, Sergeant Krause," said Lieutenant Oberman. "We are to clear the passes and kill any of the locals that offer resistance. They must be taught a lesson about our occupation of this country and that this type of behavior will be punishable by death."

"I understand sir. But something is strange here," said Krause.

"What do you mean? Do you think there are more of them hiding in the hills? An ambush?"

"I don't know how to explain it, but there is something odd—no not odd, but something wrong about this place. I've been in the service many years and I have learned to trust my instincts. Those ruins we passed on the way in, they were—"

"Spare me your instincts, sergeant. Get the men ready." The lieutenant's dismissing tone was absent of compassion.

"Yes sir." Krause exhaled his frustration. He glanced at Lieutenant Oberman. The man was short and pudgy. Just a little more than five feet tall, he weighed about a hundred eighty pounds. His face was marred with the after effects of chicken pox. Krause figured the Lieutenant had lead a life that encountered abuse at every level until it took him over and made him a giver of the same kind of abuse.

"And sergeant, I want our actions to reflect our ruthlessness. Don't kill them all at once, I want to interrogate them...slowly."

Krause acknowledged Oberman's order with a half-hearted nod, then departed to get the men ready. He hated the lieutenant—not because of his position, for he had been a soldier for many years and understood the role that officers played. But he also had seen many inexperienced officers who did not learn from the experienced sergeants—and sent soldiers to their deaths. This one, in particular, possessed some other hatred that burned within him, consuming him to kill and brutalize. This night would end badly if they were not careful.

The men were all in position shortly: Krause was thorough and his men were professionals. Oberman joined him at a vantage point where they could observe the action.

"The Serbs are all asleep and the capture should be easy enough," said Krause.

"Good. This should be a wonderful opportunity. Remember, I want them alive." He smiled in anticipation. He looked forward to interrogating the prisoners. "Give the signal."

Krause gave the signal and the men moved in swiftly. Two shots were fired that exploded the night's silence. The older Serb realized what was happening and drew a weapon. He was shot and killed. Oberman frowned as he saw that he would be denied the torture of one less Serb, but the other five were captured easily. The operation was over in less than two minutes.

THE FIVE YOUNG men sitting on the cold cave floor were petrified as their gazes darted from the Germans to each other. Those that they had come to watch for and possibly kill had overwhelmed them on their first night. Fear was accompanied by shame for their foolishness at thinking that they were anything more than just farmers.

"You are my prisoners." Oberman's voice sliced through the night's air. "If you cooperate, you shall be released, and you may return to your village and your farms."

"Lying bastard," said Josip. Oberman turned his gaze on Josip, removed his service revolver and shot Josip in the arm. Josip screamed in pain and shock as the blood flowed from the wound.

Krause turned toward his men. "I want you to reinforce the positions on the perimeter." He knew this was not necessary, but it would take them away from the butchery that would follow.

"Wait...we don't know anything!" Dimitri cried to the Lieutenant. "We are just farmers who were asked to guard the pass. That's all! We haven't even been here a day!"

Oberman looked at Dimitri, then shot him in the leg, smiling the whole time like a small child playing with favorite toys.

"I will not tolerate your Serbian lies!" Oberman replaced the revolver in its holster and removed a knife. "You shall be taught respect." He stepped toward the tied-up men; the knife blade gleamed in the glow of the fire.

"Lieutenant," interrupted Krause, "Perhaps we should wait before continuing."

"Nonsense, sergeant, the time is right," said Oberman, never taking his gaze from the tied-up men.

"Their wounds...we should tend to them and keep them alive to learn what we can." Krause lied to calm Oberman. He was sickened by the excitement in the man's eyes.

"Let them bleed. They don't know anything," Oberman said. "Sergeant, go check the men."

"I have already—"

"Check the men now!"

The sergeant looked at the bound men; the two who'd been shot were bleeding badly. Reluctantly, he left the cave.

"You bastard," Krause cursed when he far enough to not be heard. "You will get us all killed with your sickening pleasures. I will not be part of it any longer. I'm going to report this to our superiors."

Back in the cave, Oberman moved in with his knife and began to slash the three prisoners who had not been shot. The screams of the men sent eerie chills into the night air as their blood flowed onto the cave floor.

"LEAVE THEM there to die," said Oberman. "We are done here."

Krause looked at the bloodstained uniform of the officer with revulsion. His hands were covered with blood from the beatings and stabbings he had administered. He was glad he had dispersed the men into the surrounding area so they wouldn't see grotesque undertakings of the officer.

Oberman used his canteen to wash his hands of the blood. He saw that the sergeant was watching him with a look of disgust on his face.

"You don't approve of me or my actions do you, Sergeant Krause?" he asked with indifference.

"No," Krause said, purposely not using the word "sir." He continued, "You are angry and you take it out on these men who are nothing but farmers. If word should get out, or if the bodies are found, it only makes for a harder occupation when there is bad blood from this kind of action."

"Makes it harder," Oberman said incredulous. "What do you think this is...a picnic? This is war, Sergeant Krause!"

"Even in war, Lieutenant Oberman, there is honor on the battlefield."

A scream erupted from the darkness. Another followed, shattering the calm of the night. Gunfire sounded from another direction, which added to the confusion as to the direction of the attack; it was all around them. Oberman and Krause drew their weapons and took cover amongst the rocks as they scanned the area for signs of movement.

"The men, where are they?" asked Oberman.

"They took positions encircling this area. Nothing could have got past them," answered Krause.

The screaming continued, punctuated by gurgling sounds. The sporadic gunshots continued from all directions. Krause knew what was happening to his men; they were being killed one by one. Eerie silence engulfed the two men. They looked at each other.

"What do you think?" asked Oberman, his voice quavering with fear.

"I think all the men are dead," said Krause. "Just like we will be soon. I knew something was not right about this place. Evil is here, my instincts were right all along."

"What are you talking about?" Oberman shouted at him.

"I tried to tell you earlier but you wouldn't listen. At first I thought it was just from you. But it's not. There is something else here. Something much worse."

"You fool! Get hold of yourself!"

"You're scared, aren't you? You deserve to die a miserable death. I prefer to die with my men." Krause ran off into the darkness with his gun drawn. Shots rang out followed by a short scream, then silence.

Oberman sat alone, the hand that held his revolver shook. It was cold but he felt a numbing sensation along the back of his neck. He turned his head to find himself only feet away from another man. The man was tall but not large, and carried no weapons. His clothing was covered in blood, his face was covered with the crimson color that looked almost black in the dim light of the dying fire. He had the dark and hawk-like features of the local peasants, like the ones he had butchered with his knife only minutes ago,

"Who are you? What do you want? I have a gun and I will kill you!"

The man said nothing as he clamped his hands around Oberman's throat so quickly that he had barely noticed until he felt the icy cold fingers pressing into his flesh. Oberman pressed his pistol into the man's chest and fired his weapon, continuing to squeeze the trigger even after the magazine was empty. Oberman smelled the singed cloth from the bullets as he watched in horror. The man never wavered.

The face of the man was close now and Oberman could smell foulness like rotting flesh as the man breathed on him. He tried to move but the attacker's strength was tremendous, he threw all his weight into his frantic attack, but the attacker did not budge.

In an instant he was lifted by his throat and carried to where the glowing embers of the fire still burned, casting an eerie glow of light. As they approached he saw with horror that his attacker's face was smeared with blood and he had fangs that protruded several inches from his mouth. Oberman felt his bladder let go.

"You are the scum of the earth," the creature said, "I kill for a reason, you for the sheer enjoyment of it. Your sergeant was right about you. You do deserve to die." He tore the head of the Lieutenant from his body. The sound of ripping flesh and bone echoed in the eerie silence. He cast the rest aside and headed toward the cave.

CHAPTER 4

DIMITRI OPENED his eyes expecting to see the cave and the German torturer in front of him. Instead he found himself lying on a rock slab in an expansive underground area illuminated by torches and candles. The air was thick with the smell of damp earth and burning pitch of the torches. The rock walls were lined with shelves crowded with books, their bindings worn and tattered in evidence of age.

He tried to raise his head and was rewarded with searing pain that made his eyes water. Darkness engulfed him and he dreamt.

He was back in the canyon with Josip again. His gun jammed and the bear charging at him just as it had happened before. This time the bear looked different: it was smiling at him. *It will kill me this time. I will not escape death again.*

When the pain subsided he opened his eyes. Someone had attempted to bandage his wounds; he didn't think it had been the Germans, but whom then?

Carefully moving his head to the side, he saw his four compatriots lying on similar rock slabs. They looked as bad as he felt; their clothes bloodstained, their skin pale. Their wounds were also shabbily bandaged. He looked around at this place he found himself in. The furnishings were sparse and simple. The furniture was old, made of thick oak wood. Carpets covered areas of the dirt floor, their age and use evidenced by their frayed appearance.

Dimitri heard a sound. He looked toward the area of darkness where he perceived it had come from, but saw nothing.

"You're dying," the voice startled Dimitri. He turned his head and saw a man looking at him. He was dressed in simple clothing; he was tall and broad-shouldered. Dimitri couldn't guess his age, but his face was long and possessed the features characteristic of his native people. He could have easily passed for an inhabitant of his own village.

But the similarities ended with the eyes. The flames of the torches danced within them but Dimitri saw something within them he had never seen before. They glowed like a hot ember, the red-velvet illumination both enticing and fearful at the same time.

"Am I?" Dimitri asked. But he knew that already. Perhaps this was his angel come to comfort him in his last minutes of life.

"Yes, the blood loss is too great. You are all in the same condition. I tried to do what I could, but time is against you," he said sorrowfully.

"Who are you? What happened to the Germans?" Dimitri asked as he teetered on the edge of consciousness.

"I was a soldier once, a young man like you called from the fields of food to the fields of death for the greater glory of Serbia," he said. "My name is Alexander."

"How did we get here? What happened to the—"

"The Germans are all dead; I killed them. Although as I think of it now, I should have spared some of them, they were not as evil as the one was. But I lost myself in the fervor of the kill and the smell of their blood, a bad habit I have not broken yet."

"Where are we?"

"We are underneath the ruins of what once was a monastery, a true treasury of the hidden libraries of centuries. But it doesn't matter. Your time is short, I, like you, was very near death after a battle, but something came to me while I lay in the field, bleeding to death from a bayonet wound—it came and offered me a chance to live. I thought it was an angel sent from heaven offering me another chance at life, to return home and back to the fields. It was dark and I was delirious from the loss of blood, so I thought it was my chance to come back to life. But it wasn't."

"I don't understand," Dimitri whispered. "What are you saying?"

"Do you want to live?" Alexander asked. "Do you want to breathe the air of this country, this world? Even if you had to make some sacrifices? Be feared and loathed by others? Your existence based solely upon the death of others? Could you live a life such as this?"

"Of course," Dimitri said. His eyes wanted to close. He felt cold and he wanted the warmth of sleep.

"And your friends? Can you speak for them?"

"I...of course." Everything was beginning to turn gray around him.

"Then you must do what I say. If you love life, if you want to live, you must do what I say." Alexander said with a soothing quality in his voice that relaxed Dimitri.

"Yes. I want to...live."

Alexander leaned over Dimitri, opening his mouth to reveal large teeth. He slowly bit into Dimitri's neck. Dimitri moaned as the initial incision was made but he quieted as if given an anesthetic. Alexander drank for a few moments then raised his face, the blood of Dimitri on his lips, the glow of his eyes even stronger.

"You must do what I say," he said again in the calm tone, his voice possessing a hypnotic ambiance to it.

"Do as you say," Dimitri answered dreamily, his eyes glazed.

Alexander bit into his own wrist and watched as droplets welled at the wound. He placed it over Dimitri's mouth.

"If you want to live, you must drink."

Dimitri reacted to the command and sucked at the wound. His body lurched at the copper-like taste but he fought the revulsion as the words of Alexander reverberated through his mind. *If you love life, if you want to live, you must do what I say.*

Dimitri felt a surge of cold run through his body, chasing the warmth that had nurtured it for all these years. He was sure his heart had stopped and he had died, but then he was brought back to his body again, as if reborn into the world.

"That's enough for now," Alexander said. "The process has begun. I must now tend to the others. Rest now as the changes take over your body. When you awaken, we shall talk about your new life."

"New life..."

"Yes. Your new life where the night shall become your day, and the day shall become your night, and where death is bountiful in both."

TIME PASSED in a blur for Dimitri. He was not sure if he dreamt or if the events had actually happened. He remembered Alexander, the man who had saved them from the Germans and how he had brought them to this place. He remembered him saying that they were underneath the ruins of the monastery, in the catacombs that the monks had dug out as a place of refuge.

Dimitri felt weak, but his pain was gone. He sat up from the stone table. When he examined his leg where he had been shot, he saw that the wound was healed leaving only a minor blemish on his skin. He wondered how it could have healed so quickly, unless he had been unconscious a very long time. He also found that he was starved, but unsure of what he wanted.

"Dimitri," Josip called, startling Dimitri. "You are awake?"

"Yes, how are you, Josip?" He walked to where Josip sat on another slab of stone. He looked pale but otherwise fine, the wound in his arm healed.

"Okay. My wounds, they are all healed."

"As are mine." Dimitri glanced around the cavernous area. "What about the others? Franjo, Andre and Iliga?"

"They are fine," Alexander said. Dimitri and Josip were surprised because they did not hear him enter the room. "They are in another area, still resting."

"We owe you our lives," Dimitri said. "We would be dead right now if it weren't for you. How were you able to heal us so quickly?"

"You may change your mind after we talk. Come and sit." Alexander directed them to a table with chairs.

"You all were nearly dead, there was only one thing I could do to save your lives. I took your human lives and made you as I am. One who walks the night and hides from the light of day."

"Dead? Walks the night? I mean no disrespect sir, but why do you jest about such things." Dimitri wondered if this man had truly saved their lives. Josip touched his arm and Dimitri saw the questioning look in his face.

"I do not jest. I will prove it. Do you remember the stories? The creatures who drink of blood and are unable to be seen in a mirror?"

"Yes, I have heard such stories," said Josip. Dimitri nodded.

"There is a mirror on that wall, go and look." Alexander indicated the smooth glass hanging on the rock wall. Dimitri and Josip walked to the location and stood in front of the mirror. They saw light images of themselves, barely noticeable.

"I can see something," Dimitri said as he squinted and looked. "The light is poor in this cavern."

"It is good enough to see the truth. You see the faint image of what you were," said Alexander. "Soon that will be gone." He walked behind them. Dimitri and Josip looked into the mirror again, but it was empty with only the books on the back wall visible.

"A trick?" Josip said.

"No trick." Alexander gestured toward the nearby table. "There is some cheese, are you hungry?"

"Yes," said Dimitri. His mind was trying to comprehend what he was hearing and seeing.

"Eat it then."

Dimitri went to the table and sliced two pieces of cheese. He handed one to Josip and picked up the other. He raised it to his mouth. He was overwhelmed with extreme nausea at the thought of eating such a thing. He dropped the cheese. Josip did the same.

"I can't," Dimitri said. "I don't understand. I am hungry!"

"Me, too," added Josip.

"You are hungry for blood," Alexander said as he cut his wrist with a knife and drained a few drops of blood into two small cups. Dimitri and Josip watched in fascinated horror.

Dimitri's senses smelled something. It reminded him of the sweetness of a woman's strong perfume.

Alexander moved the two cups toward them, so that they were within their grasp.

Without hesitation, Dimitri and Josip picked up the cups, consumed the contents, licking every possible drop, and set them down on the table. Dimitri was shocked by his actions, yet felt growing warmth inside of him.

"Mother of God. This cannot be," he said incredulous. "The walking dead?" He looked at Josip.

"No, not exactly," said Alexander. "The term vampire describes you better. You are alive. Your only requirement to live will be to nourish and sustain your body on the live blood of animal or human. The only way you can die is to lose your head, go out in the sunlight, or drink the poisoned blood of a dead thing."

"This is for real?" asked Josip.

"Oh yes, quite real," Alexander said. "I'll be honest with you, after all your circumstances were extreme at the time. You may not want this kind of life. I have heard that there are those who go mad after a while and just kill themselves rather than making the adjustment to the new way of life."

"We cannot go home to our families," Dimitri said sadly. "Our villages would no longer accept us."

"Probably not. Some who, if they know you, will believe you are not a threat. For a while, I visited those who I knew I could trust. Then they grew old and died—another fact that you must accept. It is safest to let your family believe that you were killed, allow them to grieve your death, than to imagine you as a creature of the night. Society has condemned our lives to the dark side. People will always fear and associate us with terrible happenings. Perhaps, someday, they will see us as just creatures who roam this Earth, but that day is still a long way off."

"How have you managed to live...like this?" Dimitri asked.

"It's a long story that began a long time ago. I fell in battle during the uprising of 1804. As I said earlier, I was dying just like you, lying on the battlefield near death, my blood flowing freely from a bayonet wound in my chest. A creature came to me and promised me life and I grabbed at it. I didn't care about the consequences."

"You are more than one hundred years old!" Dimitri's mind raced with possibilities of his new life, unsure of what to believe.

"I am one hundred and thirty-five-years old. I was twenty-five when I fell in battle. I have lived here most of the time, as you have seen there are volumes and volumes of books here that contain various subjects to hold my interest. Even after all these years, I have barely touched half of them. I travel to other areas when I grow restless. That is how I found this place," he said indicating their surroundings.

"And you drink the blood of humans?" asked Josip.

"Some. But mostly I live off of cattle and wild animals. When I must take a human, I only take those who are near death or who will not be missed, the drunks or the vagabonds. You must remember that your life depends on the secrecy of your existence. To draw attention to yourself is to flirt with death. Whether you continue to live or die, the blood that you choose will dictate your future. But I don't want to confuse you with too much information all at once. That is the one benefit that you will have that I did not."

"What benefit?" Dimitri asked.

"The creature that made me, left that same night. I had to learn what I was through trial and error," he said. "I was horrified and sought shelter from those that I knew, and some of them were not very congenial. But we can talk more about this later; it is time to feed before the sunrise so that you can regain your strength."

Startled, Dimitri looked at Alexander wondering how he knew what time of day it could possibly be; he did not possess a timepiece.

"You learn how to *feel* the time of day," Alexander said, surprising Dimitri. "You also learn to sense many things." Dimitri nodded, but he didn't really understand.

"I have some cattle outside in a pen. For some reason, animals adapt quickly to us. I have an understanding with them," Alexander said.

Dimitri and Josip looked at each other in confusion.

"It's a bit of humor," Alexander said smiling "Did you think you lost your sense of humor as well?"

Dimitri and Josip both managed a weak smile.

"I keep them well fed. They are used to me feeding off of them. But as with humans, you must be careful to not take too much or you will kill them and possibly injure yourself. That is a the most important rule you must remember, do not take the blood from an animal or human that is dead, or so close to death that you may—how can I explain it—be drawn into them and their death. Do you understand?"

Dimitri and Josip numbly nodded again as Alexander rose. "What of the rest?" Dimitri asked. "Franjo, Andre, and Iliga?"

"You will come back and get them in a little while," said Alexander, "but you should know, they were much closer to death than you or Josip."

"What does that mean?" Dimitri asked.

"The process seems to react differently depending on how close the person is to actual death. It varies, but sometimes it appears to affect the outgoingness or the shyness of an individual, perhaps even the personality. It all depends how they were in life. If someone was shy or outgoing, the process may have amplified those attributes. We will have to watch them and see what happens."

"Have you—made others before?" asked Dimitri.

"No. I have avoided doing so."

"Why?"

"It's a philosophical issue I have not come to terms with. It's hard to explain."

"But us? Why the change?"

"It seemed the right thing in this case. Your deaths were from an evil and cruel man. If not for him, you might have lived."

"So how do you know these things about the process?"

"There are others I have met in my travels. Our kind are drawn together for short periods of friendship. But our survival depends on being alone or in small groups. It is easier to stay hidden."

As Dimitri followed Alexander outside into the dark and cool night air, his feelings for his friends troubled him. He had been responsible for their safety and thereby their lives. But did he have the right to make the decision for them to live a life such as Alexander had described? For a moment, he wondered if death would not have been better and simpler for him and his friends.

The darkness and coolness of the air felt exhilarating after spending so much time underground and drove his worries from his mind. Their senses came alive with the sounds of the night; they saw everything differently and were more in tune with everything around them. Alexander saw their reactions and acknowledged their realizations.

"You will be more aware of your surroundings in all respects. It will take a while to get adjusted to it but you will in time. Here are the cattle. I know it will be hard for you the first time, as it was for me. Just give in to it and let it your hunger lead you."

Alexander moved to the first cow and rubbed its neck with his hands as if stroking the animal into a sense of calmness. As the cow relaxed, he moved his face to its neck and gently sunk his teeth to it. The cow did not stir or react in a threatened manner; instead it calmly stood and allowed him to do as he pleased.

Dimitri became aware of the scent of the blood. Its smell was driving him into a frenzy that insisted his body partake in what only moments ago he had considered an act of revulsion and one that could not possibly be for him. He moved without any sense of willing his body into motion.

He motioned for Josip to follow. In an unspoken acknowledgement they singled out a cow and began the same process as Alexander. Dimitri relaxed the animal and allowed himself to be drawn to the tender flesh. Two of his teeth elongated in response to his craving the blood. Slowly he bit the animal and began to draw its blood. His mind languished at the warm substance as it flowed through his body. Out of the corner of his eye, he saw Josip performing the same actions as him.

Any thoughts that Dimitri had about death and choosing the correct path vanished as he bathed in the warmth of the blood. He felt a heightening of his senses, as if his mind was opening to things that he had only imagined before, but now seemed to be close to reality. He felt the large heart of the beast beating as it surged the blood into his mouth. Each pulse increased his awareness and allowed him to explore the uncharted areas of his mind. Death would be such a waste, he thought. The beating grew louder in his mind....

"Enough!" Alexander screamed. They released the animal. Dimitri was shocked as Alexander's voice reverberated through his mind with a strength that shook him. He saw Josip also cringing and assumed he had experienced the same. At first Dimitri felt fear at the power Alexander displayed with his command. Would he be their master and they his dominions? Would this be the price that they had paid by the creation of what they now were?

"No. Do not fear," said Alexander.

"You know our thoughts?" asked Josip.

"No. I sense your fear. I will not be your master, but your teacher. You must learn that the key to your lives is moderation in everything you do. You do not want to draw attention to yourselves. You must learn this if you are to survive." Alexander turned to Dimitri. "You have made the decision for your band of men, now I want you to go and get your comrades and instruct them as I have you. Make sure they understand, for if they fail, you fail, and it will cost your lives."

CHAPTER 5

1941

THE SIX MEN returned to the monastery in urgency as the artillery shelling of the area continued and as the oncoming troops came closer. They had known of the approaching armies and had been making final preparations to hide the opening to their underground home.

"It won't be much longer until they are on us," Dimitri said to Alexander. "They mean to take over all of this area. Before it was just the Germans, now it is the Germans and the Italians."

"All things pass in time," Alexander said calmly. "The people come and go, but in the end the Serbs will have it back. History has taught us this much so far, you will have to get use to that fact."

"It is still the patriotism in me, in all of us," Dimitri said as he indicated the others.

"There is a time to fight the evil in the world and there is a time to just let it be," Alexander said. "On the grand scheme of war, it would mean nothing, just more dying on the human behalf to appease the evil gods of war. But in a smaller scale, it would most likely tip the balance in the favor of humanity if the evil could be removed."

"And of our humanity? Where do we fit?"

A shell exploded closer than any previous ones.

"This is not the time or place for me to lecture. The enemy shells are getting closer, a sure sign of approaching troops."

"You have learned much over these past years," he began as he placed his hand on Dimitri's shoulder, "with slyness and cunning, you and your group will live for a very long time and you will see the coming of our country."

"You speak as if you will not be there to see it with us," said Dimitri, the sincerity in his voice evident of his concern. His feelings for Alexander were as great as the feelings he had many years ago for his own paternal father.

"One never knows for sure, but I have my suspicions."

"I detect a hidden meaning to your thoughts."

"You know me too well," said Alexander "War is an ugly thing in more ways than one. If you are not careful, you will use it as an excuse to feed on the humans. It will instill the desire to always feed on humans. You will think of them as nothing more than a food source, rather than what you once were—and that would be your downfall."

"You have told us all about the temptation many times. Why are you so worried about it now?"

"Because I have seen those that have fallen to it. They became reckless and careless thinking they were indestructible. Human blood makes you more powerful, but it also inflates your ego, makes you feel superior. When you think you are untouchable, you become sloppy and the locals learn of you. They have their ancient books that tell them of the old myths and legends of our kind. They go to their books from their ancestors and find information about what can be used against us. There are such things, but we are not able to look upon the words on the paper without causing pain to our eyes. They are written in the light of day and cannot be looked upon by eyes that can only see in the darkness of night."

"Philosophical?"

"No, just one of the realities that is imposed upon us. There are certain things that I cannot explain, they just are. Why do you always search for more than what is there?"

"It's in my nature."

"It is good to question our roles in this world. But for now, just accept it as fact. Philosophical issues are best left for debate, not to be tested."

"I understand," said Dimitri. "These books, are there not any in our library?"

"No. But believe me, they exist. You have been out in the fields and smelled the foulness in the air. They spread their elixir sometimes after we steal a cow. Do not believe that they don't know we are here because we do not sense them. That would be a fool's mistake. We have a unspoken agreement with the villagers."

"What should we do?"

"Instead of stealing, we shall go to town at night and buy the cattle when we need it. I am sure our money will be welcomed, and a little extra over the agreed purchase price will remove any inhibitions of doing business at night. That would solve..."

Their senses came alive and alert; danger lurked nearby, something was about to happen. They all raised their heads as if smelling the scent on the breeze, sensing the direction of the danger.

"We must go—now!" Alexander exclaimed. But it was too late to reach the underground shelter. Alexander cursed himself for dawdling out here discussing philosophy instead of paying more attention to what was around them when the Germans sprang from the woods, their guns firing wildly as intermediate shelling burst around them.

"The fools!" Dimitri exclaimed, "They attack while their own bombs rain death upon them."

"Never mind that now!" screamed Alexander. "They have found us and our sanctuary, they must be driven off!"

The bullets fell harmlessly around them and into them causing no damage to their bodies. The Germans, still lost in the confusion of the uncoordinated attack in the dark, did not realize their enemies were impervious to their bullets.

"Immobilize them," ordered Alexander. "Do not kill unless you have to!"

Dimitri and his group did as they were told, the orders of Alexander still had an hypnotic affect of obedience upon them. They made quick work of the men, using their strength and agility to subdue the attackers. Several lay upon the ground unconscious as others who had witnessed the creatures resistance to bullets, began a flailing retreat.

An intense feeling of impending danger struck Dimitri. He turned toward Alexander just as one of the remaining Germans fired an explosive round at him. Time came to a near standstill as Dimitri saw the round travel toward Alexander, but he could do nothing. Even his speed could not best the velocity of the weapon. To attempt would cost them both their lives. Alexander looked toward Dimitri and acknowledged his concern with his usual expression of warmth.

Stay where you are. You are ready to live your life on your own terms now. To live is everything....

The projectile exploded at point blank range. Alexander's body was blown apart.

"No!" Dimitri cried.

Unfrozen from the torture of time, Dimitri awoke with a rage that overcame all reasoning. He captured the German that had fired the shot and lifted him off the ground. Rage consumed him as his fangs extended to their maximum capacity. He wanted this man to know that he was going to die a miserable death.

"No...no..." yelled the German, seeing the creature that held him in its true nature. Dimitri smiled at the man's realization of his death.

"Please..."

"You dare to beg for your life!"

Holding him by the neck with one hand, he tore the man's right arm off and held it in front of him, the fingers still twitching with life.

The soldier screamed.

Dimitri tossed the arm to the ground, then tore the remaining one from its socket slowly, relishing each snap of bone and the tearing of muscles and flesh.

The soldier's eyes closed. Dimitri tossed him on the ground and began slapping him over and over trying to revive him. He knew he wasn't dead and Dimitri wasn't done either. He wanted this man alive long enough to experience more agonizing pain. The soldier's eyes fluttered open. Dimitri smiled.

"You think your angels will come for you soon, but you will not see them. I deny you that privilege for what you have done." Dimitri dug his fingers into the man's eyes and tore them out of their sockets.

When Dimitri had finished, he looked around him and discovered the others had also exhausted their fury. The area was covered in blood and parts of bodies were strewn about like a poorly managed junkyard. His men were covered in the blood. Dimitri realized they had taken part in a feeding frenzy.

Dimitri focused on the blood that covered their faces.

"How can you drink the blood of these foul men? The killers of our beloved teacher and mentor?"

They looked downcast. Dimitri's words shamed them.

"I will take no part of this." He knelt at the pile of white phosphorus that was all that remained of Alexander. He scooped them up and held his hand out to the night breeze and let the wind carry them away.

"Good-bye my friend. I will do as you have taught us and hope that we will find our place in this world where we can live in peace."

As the last ashes left his hand drifted off into the troubled night air of a country lost in its turmoil. Dimitri returned to the sanctuary beneath the monastery as the others followed, hiding his red-tinged tears.

1958

IDRIZ LAUPKI, the seven-year-old son of Alexi and Lipska, watched the commotion in his home's kitchen as his parents and grandparent's added ingredients into a large pot on the stove. The chaotic frenzy in which they worked scared the little boy. They moved with an intense nervous purpose and he saw that they were worried.

Children in the village learned to accept responsibility at an early age. Idriz knew something bad had happened. The people were scared. As farmers they were always concerned about weather, crops, and their livestock. But he had never seen them as frightened as they were now.

He knew that several cattle had been found dead with mysterious puncture wounds on their necks. His grandparents had arrived and brought an old book, its binding almost crumbling at the touch. The condition of the book reminded him of his grandparents; in many ways they were alike. Their skin was lined with wrinkles like the inside of a tree that revealed its ancient age to the world.

Now they cooked a dark liquid in a large pot. Its smell reminded Idriz of a dead animal that lay rotting in the fields. But the smell was not the worst of it. He'd seen some of the ingredients that went into the strange brew. The cattle owner brought the clear large jug. The liquid inside was a scarlet red. Idriz knew that it had to contain blood. When it was poured out of the bottle, its terrible odor had a coppery scent.

His family said prayers he had never heard before, as they added the ingredients into the pot and stirred. At some point of agreement between the group, they decided that whatever it was they were making was complete, and poured the mysterious liquid into several jugs. The bottles were loaded into a wagon and driven off.

With an apparent relief that their task was completed, the four people sat down in exhaustion and drank a combination of whiskey and coffee. Their words were few and soon they went off to rest. During this time, Idriz's father came outside of their small home to smoke a cigarette before going to sleep.

"There you are, Idriz," his father said. "I was beginning to wonder where you went."

"I have been here the whole time. I saw what you were doing," he said watching his father as he exhaled a large plume of smoke.

"You have questions, my son?"

"What was it and why was it made? I saw the bottle of blood. It scared me like an awful secret, like something evil."

"What we have done is not evil," he said as he patted Idriz's head then ruffled his hair in a playful and loving gesture. "We planned to tell you in a few years about the stories that have been passed down from generation to generation. But I guess now is the proper time since you have seen what we had to do to protect us and our friends."

"Protect?"

"Yes. We've made an elixir to ward off the evil and to protect the villagers and our animals."

"Is there an animal attacking the cattle?" Idriz asked.

"In a way, it is an animal, but then it is so much more," he said struggling to find the words to use. "It is evil in the shape of a man. It comes in the night to steal the blood from the animals. Sometimes it steals from the people, too."

"Is it a werewolf?" Idriz asked, his eyes wide.

"This beast is called the vampire and it is very real."

"Why has it come?"

"I don't know, my son. Perhaps the fighting in the mountains has forced it out of its lair."

"Can it be killed, the terrible beast?" Idriz asked.

"Yes, there are ways. We made a special elixir that will keep it away. It's a poison to the creature; if it gets inside the body it will kill it. If you splash it on them, it will burn."

"What do you call this?"

"We just call it elixir. Its ancient name means 'death to those that are already dead.'"

"And it works, you are sure?"

"Yes, it works my son."

"It drinks the blood? All of it?"

"If it plans to feed on the animal or human for a long time, it will drain the blood slowly, like saving food for a cold hard winter. If it does not care about saving, it can drain the body dry."

"Where is this creature? Is it here in the village?"

"Not in the village, but somewhere in the mountains. You know the place they call Devil's Grip?"

"Yes."

"We think it is there, but we are not sure."

"We should kill it and all that are like them. Shall we do that, Father?"

"It is not easy. It only comes out at night, and is extremely powerful and quick. The key to destroying it is to find out where it sleeps during the day. It hides from the sunlight; the light will kill it."

"Sunlight?"

"Yes, the light is deadly. Some say it is because it is God's light."

"But," the boy began unsure, "is not the moonlight from God also?"

"I think so. It is very confusing at times, even to someone like myself. Just like the books tell us something else, that I do not understand."

"What is that father?"

"That we should not kill them, for they serve a purpose."

"What purpose do they serve that is possibly good?"

"Some believe everything that is written in these old books, but I do not. When you get older and if you should choose to read them, you may also not agree with them. But there are those who agree with the idea that creatures are necessary as long as their numbers are kept small."

"If all they do is kill animals and people, why should they live?"

"Some people, in the eyes of others, do not deserve to live and if the creatures take them, the rest of us will be better off in the end."

"Who deserves to die in that manner?"

"You know how sometimes we judge people by the way they act or by the way they look? We see people who do evil but cannot prove it so that they can be punished. Instead they banish these people from town and send them to the mountains."

"Yes."

"The creatures will judge them and decide their fate. If they are to die then they will be killed."

"To kill is all right?"

"Some believe that by letting the creatures kill, they themselves have not committed any crimes against God."

The boy thought about that for a few seconds as he looked at the sky. Then he turned toward his father. "But is not keeping evil the same as being evil?"

"Yes, my son. I think so. But you must decide within yourself."

"Then I think these creatures should all be destroyed. Every last one of them," Idriz said.

His father chuckled at the determination of his young son and patted his head again, then threw away his cigarette.

"I'm going to go to sleep now. You come in a little while, okay?"

"Yes, Father." Idriz kissed his father good night. As he sat on the stone wall, Idriz's gaze turned toward the mountain in the direction toward Devil's Grip.

"You better stay up there," he said and spit in that direction. "Or I will kill you all."

1966

FIFTEEN-YEAR-OLD Idriz returned home from his trip to the

mountains. He whistled as he walked because he was in a good mood. It had been a successful hunting trip; he had gotten several deer and was bringing home a lot of meat tied on the backs of his packhorses. His father would be especially proud of this accomplishment; the fresh meat would feed them throughout the winter.

As he approached his home in the fading sunlight, he saw many people near his house and heard women wailing. He dropped his lead ropes on the packhorses and ran the remaining distance. Someone from the crowd stepped forward to meet him; it was the mayor, Lexi Aristhmiski.

"What's happened?" Idriz cried. "Where are my mother and father?"

"Idriz, something terrible has happened," the mayor began, his low voice characteristic with his short and pudgy shape. Idriz had always despised the man for he was lazy and used his position to get out of work.

"What? Tell me!"

"Your mother and father. They're...dead."

"No! No!" He felt his body's strength leave him. The mayor grabbed him by the arm and supported him, but Idriz brushed him away in contempt.

"What happened?" Idriz asked as he struggled with his emotions.

"They were mauled by an animal, perhaps a pack of wolves," the mayor said, avoiding Idriz's eyes.

"Wolves? Here in the village?"

"No, not here. They were at Devil's Grip when it happened."

"Devil's Grip? What were they doing there?"

"They went there because there were more cattle mutilations," the mayor said. "The trail led them to that area. They found nothing but thought it best to spread some of the elixir in the area as a warning. After that, we can only assume that the animals attacked them, maybe something to do with the smell of the elixir. You know its main ingredient?"

"Blood, from a dead animal," Idriz answered. "Their bodies...they weren't drained of blood?"

"We don't think so. There was a lot of blood in the area where they were attacked—that is why we do not believe it was the creature."

Idriz looked at the mayor cautiously, unsure if the inflection in his voice indicated lies or grief.

"But it might have been made to look that way," Idriz said more to himself than to the mayor. "Where is my grandmother?"

"She is inside."

Idriz moved through the crowd as the people he'd grown up with touched him and spoke their condolences. He ignored them and entered the house. He found his grandmother in her little room, sitting in her rocking chair and staring toward the mountains.

"Grandmother," he said. She looked to him, her eyes and face looked even older now in the dying light of the day.

"Idriz," she said as she raised her arms to him. He went to her and they embraced.

"It's horrible, what has happened," he said. "I will go after the animals that did this."

"They are not animals, Idriz."

"But the mayor...Lexi said that there were animals."

"The mayor says what he must to stem a panic. He is a coward."

"So it was the vampires?"

"Yes," she said. "Your father and mother were out too late and must have been surrounded by them. I told them to stay away from that area, it was too close to their...home."

"Why were they there?"

"There were more cattle killings, so your father said it was enough and set off to wipe them out. 'To kill them all,' he said. Your mother was scared he would get him into trouble by doing something foolish. She wouldn't let him go by himself—so she went with him."

"You didn't try and stop them?"

Idriz remembered the conversation he'd had with his father eight years ago. The words sounded remarkably like the words that he himself had used. Had he not said the same thing? To kill them all?

"I tried to dissuade him but they wouldn't listen. Your father said he didn't care what was in the old books about keeping a balance. He said he was tired of condoning the evil that walked in the night."

Idriz became silent with his grief as his grandmother stroked his hair with her old hands.

"I will go and finish the job," he said.

"No! I will not lose you to this foolishness."

"I'm going. Nothing will stop me."

"You must not go."

"You do not want revenge against these creatures?"

"They can wipe out the entire village if you make a mistake. We are not even sure if it is one or many. And if one should escape, we would be doomed to live in fear the rest of our lives. Do you want that on your conscience? There is a delicate balance here. Until we know exactly how many there are and where they are located, your actions will cause harm to everyone."

"Very well, I will do nothing yet, but only if you promise to help me."

"What?"

"Show me how to make the elixir," he said.

"The elixir? But it—"

"Don't worry, I will not risk the village in revenge. I promise you that. But if the time should come, I want to be ready. That is my duty is it not?"

His grandmother nodded and wept for her daughter and her son-in-law who were dead. She looked at Idriz. He was not crying. He just stared out the window toward the mountains.

IDRIZ LED THE cow down the narrow mountain path that he'd traveled countless times. He had selected this area upon his discovery of dead animals that had been discarded, which he ascertained had not been killed by animal predators. As he reached the clearing that he had chosen, he tied the cow to a tree where it could be seen easily from the area known as Devil's Grip just as the sun was getting low in the horizon.

The cow looked at Idriz's familiar face, its large eyes searching for the usual carrot that Idriz had used to win its friendship. As he stroked the animal's long and stocky neck, he felt a twinge of regret for the beast, knowing that he had used it to achieve his goal.

"Tonight we get even," he said to the cow. "I know you aren't feeling well, but that's because of the elixir I have been giving you. It will all be over soon and then I will not give you anymore...I promise."

Six months had passed since his father and mother had been buried, more than enough time to come up with a plan to get the creature that had killed his parents. His grandmother had showed him how to make the elixir and he had been feeding it to the cow so that a large amount would build up in the animal's blood system. He took extra care to insure that only he milked the cow so he could dispose of the milk and not risk harm to anyone.

It was getting darker now; it wouldn't be much longer. He found a place to hide amidst the brush and began to wait. He kept a bottle of the elixir with him in case things went wrong and he had to use it.

Without a sound, a man appeared from the woods and walked toward the tied-up cow. Idriz studied the man as best he could as the last strands of light now gave way to the moon that bathed the area with an aura of golden hue. Idriz thought it strange that there was only one. He assumed that these creatures would be like wolves and hunt in a pack. But if only one existed, that made his revenge easier.

The creature walked effortlessly, almost as if floating toward the cow, approaching the animal without any hesitation. Idriz assumed this was because it was not uncommon for stray cattle to make their way here, up from the pastures. The man caressed the cow with his hands that appeared a ghostly white in the moonlight, and then Idriz saw a flash of movement, and the man lowered his head and bit into the neck. The cow jumped briefly, but quickly settled down as if this creature soothed it in some way as it drank the poisoned blood.

Idriz recoiled with revulsion at the sight of the creature drinking the blood from the cow, but he forced himself to watch. Then came the moment that Idriz had waited for. The creature recoiled from the cow, its lower face covered with blood as it writhed in pain, tiny bits of flames erupting over its skin. It turned and disappeared from sight with a wail of pain the likes of which Idriz had never heard before. He knew it meant death.

Idriz did not pursue, for he did not see the point in it. His grandmother assured him that if the elixir was in the body, death would come and there would be no trace of the body except for a pile of ashes. The flames he had seen were evident the process had begun. He felt overwhelming delight in seeing the creature suffer.

Back in the village, he would wait to see if any more cattle disappeared to determine if more creatures existed. Then he'd decide on another course of action; he was committed to kill them all.

Idriz moved to retrieve the cow, but saw that either due to the shock, or from the amount of blood the creature drank from it, the cow now lay dead on the ground. He stroked the cow's neck, avoiding the area that had been torn open, and said a quick prayer for the creature that had helped him kill the evil being.

"Go to heaven, my beast friend, your life has been lost but we have rid the world of a creature this night, making it a better place for us all. God welcomes all good creatures, great and small and this day, you will surely be welcomed. The one that killed you will surely burn in hell."

Idriz began his trek home; his steps much lighter as the burden of revenge had now been lifted from it.

DIMITRI SENSED that something was wrong with Franjo, who had left their cavern about thirty minutes ago to scout the area, as was their custom of late upon rising, ever since the pair of humans had been discovered carrying the deathly substance. The thought of the deadly fluid brought a fleeting remembrance about the conversations he had with Alexander about the old books that held the secrets of their deaths.

He summoned the rest of the group and they headed out in search of Franjo. The last thing Dimitri needed right now was more problems as things had gradually taken a turn for the worse the past several months. Since the time that they were made, they had been content to stay in their mountains, reading the books in the extensive library, and exploring the other ruins in the vicinity.

Gradually restlessness amongst their group had begun, which could no longer be denied because Dimitri felt it himself. But what had happened six months ago had jeopardized the entire group and reflected the troubled times that had settled upon them. Their appetites had gotten out of hand, causing them to raid some of the villager's cattle in the valley below. Dimitri knew this was wrong, but his reasoning had been clouded, as had the others', by hunger. Then Franjo had gone after the two humans with such viciousness that he destroyed them both instead of scaring them off. Their custom was to avoid all contact. They had, on occasion, frightened away curious on-lookers by appearing as ghosts, but that was about the extent of their dealings with the humans.

Alexander had mentioned that this restlessness could happen and the best thing to do was take a long sleep and hope that the troubled time would pass and the humans would forget. There was a method by which they could impose a self-trance that would allow them to sleep for years. Dimitri had given this a lot of thought during the past several weeks and the likelihood of them doing it seemed even greater now.

They spotted Franjo coming toward them, screaming wildly as he clawed at the erupting bursts of flame that consumed him. They struggled with him and wrestled him to the ground as he fought and screamed. As they looked upon him, they saw his skin dissolve around his bones as the flames increased in intensity.

"A cow in the clearing...bad blood!" He screamed as he continued to writhe in horrific pain. "Don't drink! Aaahhhhhhh!"

"Franjo...Franjo!" Dimitri shouted. But it was too late. The body burst into flames, then crumbled and fell into a heap of ash that was swirled away by the evening breeze. They stared at what had been their comrade, shocked at what they had seen. Someday they, too, might die such a horrible death.

"He's gone," Dimitri said quietly. "This madness is done."

"Done?" Josip asked. "What do you mean done? We must avenge his death!"

"No. We are crazed. It is time to sleep and let the madness pass."

"We must kill the one that has done this!" Josip exclaimed and the others echoed his sentiment.

"Again, I say, no," said Dimitri. "What has been done is done. Franjo was my friend, also." He looked upon the ash-strewn ground. "Who do you think has done this? Clear the craziness from your minds and think. Do you not remember the words that the dying man said to us? Did he not beg for mercy for their son, Idriz?"

"The son," Josip said, shaking his head in acknowledgement. "Yes, it was he. He found someway to put the elixir into the animal." Then with an air of disdain he continued, "But what do we care about the words of these humans?"

The way Josip used the word *human* struck Dimitri strangely. *Had we not been human not so long ago?* "They don't know how many of us there are," Dimitri countered. "If we sleep for some years they will believe that they have killed the one creature that has spawned the myths of this place. We will be left alone."

"And when we wake?" asked Josip.

"Then we will start new again. Maybe change our location, find a new place."

The others agreed and they started toward their sanctuary where they would entomb themselves. They all seem to accept this as the right course of action to insure their survival. But Josip was not relaxing his thoughts for sleep just yet. He knew he was bound to follow Dimitri and what he had suggested, for it was for the good of the group. But in his mind, he began plotting the revenge of Franjo when he awoke; he engraved the name Idriz on his mind so he wouldn't forget it.

CHAPTER 6

Present Day

COMMANDER JOHN Reese's plane arrived at the airport of Skopje in the former Yugoslav republic of Macedonia. He found it interesting how it had been several years since he had been outside the United States on travel, and in the past twenty-four hours, he had gone from Norfolk to Florida, then stopped in Italy to refuel and now he found himself in the Balkan region of Europe.

After clearing the check-in process that was now streamlined to swiping his military identification card through a scanning device, he retrieved his one piece of luggage and was ushered to an arrival area where he hoped he would find transportation as promised to the Base Camp. An army private approached and saluted him.

"Commander, I am Private White. I've been assigned to escort you to Base Camp Bondsteel. Colonel Antol sends his regards and regrets he could not meet you personally," he said in an obviously memorized greeting.

"Nice to meet you, Private White," Reese said as he returned the man's salute. "Shall we get started? I'm sure we have a bit of a ride ahead of us."

"Yes sir, about two hours," he said as he grabbed the Commander's bag. "This way, sir."

Outside of the airport the sun shone, but the air was cool. It felt refreshing to Reese after sitting on the airplane for almost twelve hours. His bag was placed in the back of the military vehicle and they were quickly on their way.

"First time in this area?" asked White.

"Yes."

"Here to be an observer?"

Reese remembered that this whole affair was supposed to be kept quiet. His driver had been dispatched from Camp Bondsteel to pick him up and bring him to the base camp—that was probably the full extent of what the driver knew. The question offered an extremely plausible reason for him to be there, and Reese decided to go with it.

"Yes," he answered. "An observer for SOCOM. They are conducting a test of new logistical procedures in the field. They want me to check their effectiveness."

"Oh. I thought you might...well...be here for something else."

"Like what?"

"There are some rumors going around the camp about some weird murders."

"Weird?" Reese asked, trying to hide his interest.

"Some of the guys have heard talk about people being killed by creatures."

"Creatures?"

"Yes sir. Sounds crazy, doesn't it? I don't believe it though. This whole country is so old...the locals have all kinds of stories about strange beings."

"What kind of creatures?"

"Werewolves, vampires...you know, like the kind from the movies."

"Really? Has anyone actually seen one of these creatures?"

"I don't think so. I think the rumor got started when some civilian bodies were brought in to the hospital. They say the bodies were drained of all their blood."

"Did anyone see these bodies?"

"They wouldn't let anyone near the hospital."

"What else?"

"That's about it sir."

Reese thought that whether or not there was any truth to this scenario he had been sent to investigate, the small leak of information that had occurred was not cause for major alarm. However, the rumors needed to be stopped.

"Maybe they were concerned about them having some sort of infectious disease. They do have a problem here with tuberculoses. It was probably an imposed quarantine to just make sure everyone would be safe if the bodies had TB. Doesn't that sound more reasonable?"

"Yes sir."

"I'm glad to hear that you are a reasonable person, Private White," said Reese, thinking about how he could use this opportunity to stop the stories from spreading. He had seen what could happen. A few soldiers write letters home to their parents or spouses and before long, letters and phone calls assail congressmen and women asking for information, or worse, investigations. If relatives don't get satisfactory answers, they almost always go to the press and claim the military is hiding something. Then journalists start crawling out of the woodwork, looking for confirmation of the stories.

"You might want to be careful who you tell about these so-called creatures. I would hate to think that you would spread rumors about such ridiculous things. You might want to let some of the other guys know that telling stories like that can get them into trouble."

"Trouble?"

"Spreading rumors and scaring everyone. It's bad for morale. People get upset and they can't work. That's dangerous here. You don't want your buddy looking for creatures when he or she is supposed to be watching your back, do you?"

"No sir. I guess I never thought about it that way."

"You might want to let your friends know."

"Yes sir. I will."

Reese smiled and let the issue rest. He decided to use the rest of the time to familiarize himself with the area. The private had maps in the vehicle and Reese used them to plot where the incidents had occurred as mentioned in the reports. He asked several questions about the surrounding area and in that respect, the young private was quite useful. Before being assigned as the daily run driver to the airport he had made several patrols in the outlying areas. He described the ruins in fair detail and Reese marked the map as he tried to formulate what the region looked like.

He was unable to relinquish the words that General Stone had used in his note, "use of such creatures as a military asset." Did he actually believe they existed? Was he actually considering the possibilities of controlling them and using them in the military?

Reese had formulated his own opinions that history was full of myths that were nothing more than just fabricated stories or exaggerations. But he also believed that some of them held truth. If some form of creatures existed during those earlier periods and if they lived then, why couldn't they live today? But if they did, why had they not been discovered?

If creatures existed as those that had been chronicled through history, how would one even go about trying to control them? No one else had been able to. Why or how could they be controlled now? Supposedly, these creatures were fast, strong, intelligent, and had survived for hundreds of years, virtually indestructible. Realization smacked him with the force of a baseball bat to the face.

"That's it!"

"Sir?" The private asked. "I don't understand? What's it?"

"Oh...nothing. Sorry," Reese said, embarrassed. It was so damn obvious that it scared him; the perfect soldier was what the General wanted. A stealth team of creatures could penetrate any stronghold undetected. Accomplish any mission imaginable. Become the ultimate remorseless killing machine. And all Stone would have to do is point them in the right direction and let them at it.

Reese didn't like this line of thinking. He may have been handed the dream of a lifetime if these creatures actually existed, and here he was wondering about the moralistic implications of using creatures as killing machine to do the military's covert work. If they existed, weren't they killers already? Reese imagined the creatures sucking the blood out of their victims, then killing them unmercifully.

"Sir, are you all right? You look kind of pale."

"Yes," he answered, glancing at the young private as he struggled to control his stomach. "Just jet lag and this bumpy road."

"I thought maybe it was something you ate. The food on those Air Force planes is kind of..."

But Reese didn't hear the private finish his sentence as he leaned out the window and vomited.

They arrived at Camp Bondsteel as darkness captured the entire region. The camp was situated near the city of Urosevic. Massive floodlights lit the camp and its perimeter. Private White drove Reese to the base commander's office. As Reese entered the building he was led to a conference room by a staff sergeant. As he stepped into the room, Army Colonel Antol rose to meet him; Reese noticed two other people in the room.

"Commander, glad to see you made it," Colonel Antol said as he shook Reese's hand.

"Thank you, sir." Colonel Antol, a fit-looking black man, smiled warmly, but appeared haggard as if sleep had eluded him for quite some time. His shaved head glistened with sweat in the bright fluorescent light even though the temperature in the room was cool. The colonel was under a lot of stress just running the base camp under normal circumstances, but now with this added strain, it showed in his physical appearance.

"Let me make introductions." The Colonel led Reese to a fellow Naval officer who wore the trident emblem above his left pocket indicating he was a Navy SEAL. He was about six feet tall and a solid two hundred pounds. His blond hair was the traditional short length and a scar ran along his left cheek.

"Commander John Reese, this is Lieutenant Mark Johnson, SEAL Team Two commander."

"Sir," said Johnson.

Reese felt the iron grip of the man as they shook hands. SEAL Team Two was one of the teams that he provided logistical support for back on the base in Little Creek. He recognized the man's name, but had never met him before.

They moved to the next man. He was a sharp contrast to the physically fit Lieutenant Johnson. His body was short and stocky in size, his hair completely gray, but his face had that favorite uncle look to it.

"This is Major Sam Barkley, the medical officer."

"Commander," the Major said. He shook his hand. "Welcome to Kosovo."

"Thanks...I think."

"There are three other people that are involved, two are in this building," said the Colonel. "But I thought it would be better to talk amongst ourselves first. Sergeant Estefan, who was a witness to the event, is still in an incoherent state in the hospital. You'll soon meet Corporal Brosnev who is interpreter for the civilian, Idriz Laupki." Colonel Antol sat down, indicating for the rest of them to do the same. "Gentlemen, nothing said here tonight will be discussed outside the confines of this room. Is that understood?"

Everyone nodded.

"Commander, General Stone has asked that you lead the investigation and that myself and staff provide any assistance that you may require."

Reese heard a tone he did not like from the Colonel who had been congenial up to this point. He knew it would be an awkward arrangement to work in if he was in charge instead of the Colonel. It would quickly become counterproductive and precious time could be lost.

"Sir, forgive me for correcting your statement, but I was told that I would be top advisor, but not in charge of the operation. I am to provide recommendations on how to conduct the investigation and recommend action to be taken. You will have the ultimate say on what goes." Reese knew that it wouldn't matter either way; he would explain it all to Commander Scott at SOCOM and have him smooth it over so that everyone would be happy and cooperate.

"Must have been some miscommunication on my people's part," the Colonel said, as his tone became less defensive. "How do you recommend we proceed?"

"I've studied the reports. Is there any information to add at this point?"

"No. There hasn't been any change in the condition of the sergeant. We were not authorized to run a reconnaissance mission until you arrived."

"I understand your concern about scouting the site, but I would suggest not to do so until I have researched some things and gone over some...special tactics that might be required with Lieutenant Johnson. I would like to interview the civilian first. I have questions I need answered before I can recommend the next course of action."

"Okay, Commander, talk to the civilian," the Colonel said. "We'll meet later when you're ready to discuss your next move."

Reese thought that they had finished for now, but noticed the Colonel still appeared to have one more question for him. He hesitated on getting up from the table.

"Commander, we're all intelligent people here." The colonel swept the room with his hand. "What does the General think is going on here? I know what it looks like but...come on now, creatures that kill people and suck their blood? *Vampires* for God sakes—does he really believe they exist?"

Silence settled as they waited for Reese's response. But he said nothing suspecting the Colonel wasn't finished speaking. It was better to let him air out all his grievances now. "It's just local folklore. This country's history is loaded with stories such as these. You know that probably better than anyone in this room does. It was just some damn rebels that killed the civilian's children, then Captain Block got involved and he was killed. Lieutenant Johnson and his SEAL team can go in there and route the bastards out in an hour. But I can't send them because General Stone wants *you* to look at it first."

"Colonel, I don't know what we're dealing with here. I hope you're right and you can send in the SEALs to take care of it." Reese paused. "Because the other possibility scares the living hell out of me."

IDRIZ LAUPKI sat on the cot in the small room. He looked much older than his fifty years; his eyes red from anger and tears, encircled by the wrinkles in his flesh from spending too much time under the rays of the sun and facing the harsh winters in the mountains.

The land was unforgiving. If the constant fighting or weakening economy didn't claim him or his people, the lack of proper medical care and food did. But it was still his home that he had fought to keep, and would continue to do so until the land claimed him as it had his wife.

His wife, his Anna, had been a frail woman who had been claimed by the childbirth of their last daughter six years ago. He carried on with his life, grieving the loss of his wife and devoting himself to the raising of his two daughters. But now, they were all gone. He found himself tired, extremely tired. The past few days had worn him past the point of exhaustion, but he could not sleep. The return of the creatures and the murders of his children now occupied his every waking thought. His two precious girls were dead by the hands of the creatures that had killed his parents more than thirty years ago.

The creatures. So he had been wrong when, as a young man of fifteen, he thought that he had removed the dark cloud that lingered over these mountains and killed the beast. Or had he? Perhaps these creatures were not the same? Or there had been more than one? But why after all these years had his children been slain—if not for retribution for what he had done so long ago.

He had assumed that the creature he had killed was the only one. After its death, there were no more mysterious deaths of people or of animals. But maybe more than one existed, and they had moved somewhere else for a while and finally returned. He rubbed his temples. Had he taken part in the deaths of his beloved children by exacting revenge for his parents?

His daughters said that they wanted to go out and pick some berries before winter settled in. He had been busy tending the cattle and told them it was all right. He had not even thought to ask where they would pick berries. If he had known, he would have told them to not go near the old ruins. When they hadn't returned home at sunset, he went looking for them. He talked with other villagers and pieced together where Maria and Sophia had gone. The next day as the sun rose, death greeted him. Word had been brought that their bodies had been found at the ruins. He went to them and after seeing his Maria and Sophie in death, knowing how they had been killed; he went crazy with grief, wandering for a day oblivious to everything.

At first he had thought that going to the Americans for help was the right thing to do. He could not fight the creatures on his own. But now...he wondered if he had made the right choice because another man had died from his actions. He tried to warn the American captain, but the fool did not listen to him. The westerners did not know the stories, they discounted them as myths from a backwards people. They would think differently now that one of their own had been killed.

Glancing around the wooden structure they called the hospital, he was unable to leave this place. They were going to conduct some kind of investigation into what happened and were waiting for another American to arrive. The interpreter assured him that they would go and kill the creatures soon. Idriz did not care about the American that was coming and their promise to kill the creatures, for he was going to kill them no matter what happened, no matter what the cost he had to pay. It didn't matter what happened to him. He had no desire to live except to kill the creature that had killed his little girls. He would do whatever it took to see that done before he took his last breath.

COMMANDER REESE stepped into the small conference room where Corporal Brosnev and the civilian Idriz Laupki waited for him. The corporal stood and greeted Reese.

"Sir, Corporal Brosnev reporting as ordered."

The gaze of Idriz followed the action of the young corporal. Reese was momentarily caught off guard by the look in Idriz's eyes, there seemed to be so much...*life* in them. Or was it burning anger or hatred for the loss of his two children? Reese felt a sense of unease toward this man that he had not even met yet.

"At ease, corporal," Reese said as he offered his hand. "It's nice to meet you. I understand you will be my interpreter?"

"Yes sir," the corporal said as he shook Reese's hand.

"And you have been involved in this...situation since the beginning?"

"Yes sir."

"Good. Now please introduce me to our guest."

The Corporal spoke a few words and Idriz rose and offered his hand to the commander. As they shook hands, Reese noticed the man's hands were like sandpaper, but his grip was strong.

"Please offer my condolences for the loss of his daughters," Reese said before the handshake was finished. The corporal spoke and Reese immediately felt a tightening of the handshake and an understanding in the man's face for just a second.

"Thank...you," Idriz said in broken English, which surprised the interpreter, and Reese.

Reese acknowledged his thanks and indicated for them to be seated. He took papers out of his case and some maps that had been folded and refolded a dozen times. Idriz's gaze followed his movements closely, studying Reese with an intense curiosity.

"Corporal, please explain to him that I know it will be painful to talk about some of the events, but it is necessary in order to clear up this matter as soon as we can."

Corporal Brosnev quickly translated and Idriz nodded his understanding.

"I want to know about the liquid that was thrown at these creatures."

The corporal was surprised at the question and hesitated.

"Corporal, you must do it exactly as I say it and when I say it," Reese said firmly, but in a calm tone. "It is important to get honest answers. Do you understand?" The corporal nodded as he translated the question. Idriz also appeared surprised at the question, but responded to the corporal, while not taking his gaze from Reese.

"He says it is something that has been passed down through his family from the ancient books. It is meant to ward off the creatures and even kill them if they consume it."

"What are these creatures?" Reese asked. The interpreter asked the question. Idriz stared at the Commander as he answered.

"He says," the interpreter paused, "he says you know what they are."

"Tell him I want *him* to tell me what they are."

The interpreter translated the question.

"Vampyres," Idriz said in his heavy Slavic accent. "Vampyres."

Reese told the interpreter, "Tell him to start at the beginning, as far back as he can remember."

The interpreter relayed the request and Idriz began the story as Reese listened intently and made notes on the paper in front of him. He'd written:

The liquid—need more
Special equipment—get with Johnson
Delivery method—get with Barkley

Reese had read the history of this country and knew it was full of turmoil. He also knew it would be a perfect location for creatures to inhabit; with constant fighting within the country, death was nothing new, it was a way of life and some people wouldn't be missed. Many regions of the country were not inhabited by villagers and offered perfect places to hide for those who did not want to be found.

When he finished talking, Idriz appeared drained from retelling the horrible events that had happened to him during his life.

"Where did he get the elixir?" Reese asked as he scanned his notes.

"He says he made it," the Corporal responded.

"Good. Please tell him I want him to make some more. And I want you to watch him and write down everything involved in the process."

The corporal relayed the request to Idriz, who nodded, then spoke rapidly to the interpreter.

"Sir, he wants to know what you are going to do and if you believe what he has told you? Also...if you are going to kill the creatures, he wants to help."

"I'm going to arrange surveillance of the area to make sure they are still there before we...before we do whatever it is we are going to do. As to his other question," Reese carefully chose his words. "I believe what factual events have happened up to this point. As to the story he has relayed, many aspects are corroborated with some of the information I have seen and read. As far as the creatures are concerned, we are going to find out."

Reese ignored Idriz's comment about killing the creatures, if they did in fact exist. He avoided meeting Idriz's curious stare for fear that the man might see that killing the creatures was the last thing Reese had in mind.

CHAPTER 7

"HOW COULD you have been so foolish, Josip?" Dimitri asked from within their cavernous crypt as he pressed Josip against the stone wall, his anger evident. "First it was the two little girls instead of the father, and now—"

"It was for Franjo that I did it." Josip pushed away Dimitri's arms. Andre and Iliga watched in the background with their usual indifference. "The fool human suffers more this way by seeing the deaths of his daughters. Franjo has been avenged."

"And the other soldier who was snooping around?" Dimitri countered. "The American is dead. And the man that you hate so much...this Idriz...he will not stop now. He has nothing to lose because you have taken it all from him. His daughters were all that mattered to him!"

"He will die, too," said Josip. "But I want him to suffer. He will agonize over the death of his daughters."

"Have you forgotten he knows how to make the poison? The poison that killed Franjo and almost burned us. You jeopardized all of us by doing this." Dimitri rubbed his forehead as he tried to regain his composure. "We cannot expose ourselves if we are to survive. We agreed. We *all* agreed to stay away from the humans," Dimitri said as he looked at Andre and Iliga then at Josip. "We have gone to the village every couple of months to buy the cattle we need. No one suspects anything. We can go on with our lives. But now they have seen us, and there are the Westerners involved now, the Americans."

"Our lives? You call this way of life living? Hiding like animals?" asked Josip. "I am tired of the blood from the cattle. The human blood raises my awareness as it burns its way through my veins. We should feed on them, make them fear us, and respect our bidding. We can control them."

"Control them?" Dimitri said, incredulous. "You are a fool! If you think you are superior and indestructible, you will become careless and surely die. We must stay together now more than ever. Remember what Alexander told us: Beware the false power of the human blood."

Josip looked embarrassed by his comments about the blood and the humans. The words of Alexander floated in his mind with the lessons he had taught them through the centuries of life that he had possessed. Slowly his disposition softened and he nodded.

"We have entered a dangerous period in time because others have seen us," Dimitri added, glad to leave the topic of human blood.

"No one will believe the crazed fool Idriz," said Josip. "He will spin the stories and they will think that he has gone mad by the loss of his two daughters."

"That may be true, but we should still leave this place," said Dimitri.

"And return to the mountains? There is nothing there but wilderness and emptiness. We do not want to go," Josip said. "Here there are people and they interest us with their doings. There are new books and things to amuse us."

"Is this true?" Dimitri asked as he looked at Andre and Iliga. They both nodded.

"But we are not as well protected here..."

"You worry too much," Josip said. "What has been done, has been done. I may have been wrong but there is no changing what happened. The Americans will no longer bother us; we are myths and will soon be forgotten amidst all the fighting that is going on. We can make it look like the wolves tore the American apart, a freak accident. They will come and look at the body and think the same thing."

They gathered around Dimitri: Josip, Andre, and Iliga, placing their hands on him in a reassuring manner. They were a family and he was their leader. He still thought it wrong to stay, but he would acquiesce to their wishes.

"It is dark now," said Dimitri. "There are cattle in the pen. Let us drink ourselves full of life. Then we will take care of the remains of the American. They will be back soon to investigate."

LIEUTENANT MARK Johnson sat at a table in his quarters caught in the memories that continued to haunt him.

He was a skinny young boy cornered by three large boys on the playground of the high school.

"We're going to kick your ass," one of the large boys said.

"Why? What have I done to you?" Mark didn't know why he had been singled out. He'd transferred into the school only a week ago. His alcoholic father had moved to this area after losing his job, again. His mother had died years ago from cancer.

"*You don't look right,*" one of them said. "*We don't know you and you've been walking around all week with this high and mighty attitude. We think it's time you got your welcoming so you know who is in charge around here.*"

"*No, wait...please.*"

But they refused to listen to his pleas and beat him ferociously. After a while, when he could no longer stand, one of them took out a knife and cut him along the side of his face.

"*There, you're labeled now,*" one of them said and they all laughed. With a final kick, they left him lying in the blood-soaked dirt.

His father refused to listen to his "petty" problems. Johnson withdrew from all school activities. When not in school he lifted weights in his basement and went out to places that he knew the other school kids didn't hang out at. He studied martial arts at the local YMCA.

By his senior year, Johnson was in terrific physical shape. Not only had his muscles hardened, so had his personality. He had no friends and associated with other students only for school projects and class work. After graduation, unsure of what to do with his life, he saw a recruitment ad on the television for the Special Forces of the United States Navy. They were called SEALS, which stood for by the Sea, Air and Land; the manner by which they were introduced into hostile environments. He was fascinated by the organization of men that were the pride of the Special Forces for their discipline and perseverance.

The next day, he was at the recruiting office and the following week he was off to boot camp. Physically unchallenged by the basic training, he applied and passed entry test for Navy SEAL training. Once in the environment that challenged both the mind and body, he excelled and received accolades from the instructors and classmates. He even surprised himself by making friends with men who were just like him.

But he still had the dreams sometimes. He felt the knife cutting through the flesh on his face. He would awake in the middle of the night breathing hard, bathed in sweat, his hand and fingers tracing the scar. He learned to deal with this emotional hitchhiker from his past and forced himself to banish the thoughts from his mind and leave those specters behind; it worked most of the time.

His first assignment was to SEAL Team Two. After a year and a half and having done extremely well on the assigned missions, he was selected to attend a special program whereby he could attend college and apply for a commission to become an officer. Again, he excelled and attained excellent grades, graduating at the top of the class. One day in casual conversation with a fellow classmate, he was asked about his family back home.

"Family? The Navy is my family. They are the only ones that have ever cared for me and given me what I have needed. That is the family that I will die for."

"Excuse me Lieutenant?" Commander Reese said.

"Oh...sorry sir," Johnson said as he stood.

"Must have been a good thought you were having," Reese said.

"Can I help you sir?"

"I need your expertise. I'm a planner, not an operator. You're the expert in conducting covert operations so if I should suggest something that you do not feel is correct, I want you to tell me okay?"

"Yes sir," Johnson said. "What did you have in mind?'

"For starters, I want satellite reconnaissance of the area where the captain was killed, and I want it tonight."

"Shouldn't be any problem as long as the satellite is within range. I'll have to check that out." He checked the time on his watch; there was approximately eight hours until darkness. "We have unlimited use during the Kosovo ops. It can be viewed in the Command Center here in the Camp."

"Can you augment it to pick out signatures that would not be as warm as the human body? Make its reception more sensitive?"

"I should be able to get something done along those lines," Johnson answered as he looked at Reese. "But why...wait, you think there is something there, don't you? That there is some truth to all these stories."

"The facts dictate that something is there, the question is—what?"

"And if there is something there that is not...normal? Then what?"

"One step at a time, Lieutenant. You arrange for the satellite observation, I'll meet you in the command center at dusk. I have one other thing to look into. We have engineers here that can manufacture things?"

"Sure. Great bunch, tell them what you want and they make it."

"Thanks, I'll see you later," Reese said distractedly as he headed to the medical treatment facility to find Major Barkley. He found the doctor watching Idriz Laupki in one of the operating rooms. Idriz was mixing the elixir.

"Major." Reese said to get his attention.

"Commander, do you know what he is using to make whatever it is he is making? He's using blood and..."

"We can discuss the ingredients later. I need you to create something for me and I need it by first light tomorrow."

Major Barkley seemed perturbed that he was being pulled away from watching Idriz.

"Don't worry," said Reese. "The corporal is keeping track of everything he uses in the preparation."

"I think the civilian knows it, too. He's been misleading the corporal. He picks up something and acts like he's putting it in and he isn't. I can't even tell you at this point what is or isn't in it. He's a sneaky guy."

Reese frowned, but would let the issue wait until later. If they had to, they could analyze the solution to figure out its content.

"What is it that you need?" Barkley asked.

Reese tried to figure out how to describe the device he envisioned. "Imagine a device that can be controlled remotely, like from a hand device. Its function would be to inject a quantity of liquid into a body quickly."

"We have automatically controlled injectors here that dispense painkillers. They're sensitive devices and extremely precise. It would just be a matter of reconfiguring the controls to work from a hand-controlled remote. What about distance?"

"As much as I can get."

"That might be a problem. I can probably get you fifty feet or so."

"That will have to do. Now what I want you to do is imagine the injector and its contents attached to a...collar-like device."

"What? A collar? You mean like a dog collar?"

"Not a dog collar. Bigger. About the size to go around a human neck."

Major Barkley didn't say anything. He just stared at Commander Reese with a bewildered look, afraid to ask for more information.

"And make it of the hardest metal we can get our hands on here. It needs a locking device, too."

"I don't know..." said Barkley. "I'll see what I can whip up."

"Take what you need and go see Captain Souer in the machine shop. I've already talked to him and he knows you're coming. I have instructed him that he is to do exactly what you ask and complete it by first light. Do not tell him anything beyond what is absolutely necessary to manufacture the collars. Make at least a dozen of them and remember—these things must be tamper-proof. If the wearer tries to remove the collar, or if it's activated by the remote, the injector will inject the substance."

"And the substance?" Barkley asked.

Reese glanced at Idriz who was still mixing and stirring.

COMMANDER REESE entered the operations center about an hour after the sun had gone down. He walked to where Lieutenant Johnson sat, but did not say anything. Johnson watched the view screen as he typed on the keyboard.

Johnson looked up and saw Reese watching his actions. "Commander, we're just about ready, and I have been honing the system to the requirements you asked for. There is a two-minute delay in-between setting adjustments. It shouldn't be much longer."

"Good," said Reese. "I don't think we will have to wait long."

"Wait for what?"

Reese didn't answer and Johnson returned his attention to the display and continued to adjust the display requirements as the Commander had requested.

"Have you ever searched for something your entire life, then when you think you have found it, you have...second thoughts?"

"I think so," Johnson answered. "In my career I have been trained to do some unique missions. It's one thing to train for an operation but quite another to do it. They're a world apart."

"You may be in for new surprises that I am sure you have never trained for," Reese said as he rubbed his eyes. "Any coffee?"

"There is always coffee in the military," Johnson said and smiled. "But you look like some sleep will do you better."

"Later," Reese said as he went to get some coffee. "You want any?"

"Sure."

Reese returned with the coffee and sat down behind Johnson. The display showed the area of the ruins. It glowed a low luminous green color. Other areas reflected different shades and hues of the color depending upon their degree of warmth.

"You should see some heat sources in the area. I had some cattle driven in that direction."

"Cattle?"

"Food source, Lieutenant," said Reese. "Try and keep them in the field of the display, especially the ones closest to the ruins. If there is any truth to our tale, the cattle will appear as if dinner just arrived."

"Got them," Johnson said. He showed the outline of the animals to Reese using his finger to trace the images on the computer screen. Reese was amazed how the cattle were easily visible—all due to a satellite that circled the Earth hundreds of miles above. It was an interesting clash of time and history...the new being used to track down the old.

"We'll have the images for about two hours. Everyone wants to use the satellite, " Johnson said. "I had to pull some strings to get it for this long."

"If anything is going to happen, it will be soon. If the creatures do exist, they will rise and feed shortly after sunset."

"Feed?" Johnson looked unbelieving at Reese. Reese returned his gaze but didn't say anything as he sipped his coffee and watched the images on the monitor. Johnson was about to ask him again as he saw a very faint heat source register next to the cow, in the lower right corner of the display.

"That wasn't there a couple of seconds ago," Johnson said. He pointed to the screen. Just as he finished the statement, another faint spot emerged followed by two more, all of them next to the cow.

"If we were not tuned to the extra sensitivity that you wanted, you wouldn't see these. Whatever they are, they're not giving off much heat."

As seconds passed, the spots grew and began to take globular shape. The cow seemed to disappear from the screen as its warmth dissipated.

"What the hell is it?" Johnson asked as he turned toward Reese. "How can they appear and grow warmer?" Reese did not say anything; his gaze remained transfixed on the screen and the intensifying green images.

"Commander?" Johnson said. "What is it?" But as Johnson returned his gaze to the display, he clearly saw the outlines of four shapes that were distinctly human in form. "That's impossible. They were not there before."

"But they were," Reese said calmly. "You see, they did not appear on the screen in the human shape at first because there was very little heat from their bodies as they emerged from their hidden crypt. Their blood is cold and void of life. As they drank the blood from the animal, their bodies became warm and they could be detected. As time goes by, their heat will fade away as the coldness of their bodies overcomes the warmth of the newly acquired blood."

Johnson did not say anything but his thoughts resurrected images of Lestat and Louis from *Interview With A Vampire*. But he had never believed such creatures could ever exist. And now, here they were, as he watched the images move off and their green heat signatures fade away.

"Lieutenant Johnson?"

Johnson left his thoughts of vampires and returned to the present.

"Yes...I'm okay," he said. "Just caught me off guard." He returned his gaze to the screen. The satellite had moved beyond range, the screen blanked. "There has to be another explanation."

"Do you have any ideas?" Reese asked. "Is there anyway that what you have just seen could have been faked?"

"They could have..." Johnson searched for an explanation. "Maybe they were wearing heat blockers when they emerged, then removed them later."

"And the cow, did it suddenly put one of these blockers on?" Reese asked. "And for what purpose?"

Johnson looked at Reese.

"We're done here," Reese said. "I think we've seen all we need to, right?"

"Yes...I think so."

"We need to discuss some tactics on how to proceed. You're the operator, but I can share what I know about the creatures' dwelling, their habits and weaknesses. I want to be ready by 0600 for a mission briefing with the staff."

"Then what?" Johnson asked.

"We go below the ruins to where they live and find out what we are dealing with. Most importantly, we must ensure we have enough hours of daylight left, otherwise we may become the hunted."

CHAPTER 8

AT 0550 COMMANDER Reese entered the conference room at the task force main headquarters building. Major Barkley and Lieutenant Johnson were there as he requested to confirm that they were ready for the operation; Colonel Antol would arrive in a few minutes.

Last night after seeing what Reese felt was confirmation that non-human creatures lived below the ruins, it was time to move to the next phase. Lieutenant Johnson and he had discussed tactics in a general sort of way, but Reese did not want to let him know the full extent of what he had planned, even though he suspected that Johnson had his own ideas for a search-and-destroy mission.

Reese had received confirmation from Commander Scott at SOCOM that General Stone concurred with his analysis and his recommended course of action. The course of action would be dangerous, yet he felt exhilarated at the possible wealth of information he would learn. Between considering military maneuvers and his own personal desires, his thoughts thwarted any chance he'd had for sleep.

"Okay, before the Colonel gets here," said Reese, "I want to make sure we are ready..." he paused, then changed direction. "I know this all sounds weird as hell and something straight out of some nightmare from your childhood. But believe me, all indications are that we are dealing with an unknown species—some would call them vampires. What we are about to do has never been attempted."

"And what exactly are we attempting to do?" Barkley asked. Reese prepared to answer but stopped as Colonel Antol entered the room.

"Good morning gentlemen," he said in a rather gruff manner. He looked toward Reese. "Commander, I received a call from General Stone telling me that you have a plan you wish to implement."

"Yes sir," he said sensing the irritation from the Colonel, Reese knew that General Stone didn't *ask* him, but told him that he would be in charge of the operation even though Reese had asked that it be couched in a way to help maintain an air of cooperation with the Colonel. Reese took a deep breath and spoke.

"The plan is simple as long as we keep certain facts in the front of our minds. These...creatures are extremely dangerous. We know they have killed and appear to be impervious to bullets. Extreme caution must be emphasized."

"Commander," Colonel Antol, began, "We have plenty of ordinance here to wipe them out regardless if they are...vampires. It seems a straight-forward issue about how to deal with them."

"We are not going to destroy them. We are going to capture them." Reese said in a casual tone.

"Capture?" Johnson asked almost in perfect synchronization with the Colonel. Major Barkley looked much less surprised about the statement because he had surmised as much from the instructions that Commander Reese had given him in the design of the collars.

"That's right," he repeated. "Our orders are to capture the creatures...alive." Reese let the silence settle upon the room before continuing. "We are to subdue them for transport back to the United States under the tightest security."

"And I assume you are going to tell us how we are going to do this?" Colonel Antol asked in an abrupt tone indicating his disagreement with the plan.

"Yes sir. We have quantities of the elixir made by Idriz. We also have a confirmed report from Corporal Brosnev that the liquid did have a detrimental effect on the creatures when it was thrown at them. So we assume that the mixture can be used as a weapon against them."

"If any of this nightmare is true, you are gambling Commander," said the Colonel.

"There is a backup plan that I shall also explain, sir."

"Continue then."

"Major Barkley has developed a device that will be placed around the neck of each creature. The device contains the solution with an automated release mechanism that will inject the elixir into the creature if needed and kill it. The mechanism is controlled by a remote device which shall be held by a protected guard in the event that the creatures attack."

"I don't think that these creatures will place these devices on freely," said Johnson.

"No. If they are aware of what we are trying to do, they will destroy us. That is why we must do this today, in the daylight. We would have no chance in the hours of darkness when they are awake. They sleep during the day and are susceptible to attack."

"So," said Johnson, "the plan is to sneak in on them today, slap the collars on them and move them out in darkness? It's that simple."

"That's the plan, although I would not call it simple. One mistake and the whole team can be wiped out. No conventional weapons, with few exceptions, will harm the creatures. If anyone starts going crazy, the whole operation will be over in seconds."

"How do we kill them if the collars do not work?" asked Barkley.

"The men will be armed with sprayers filled with the elixir. If they don't work, we will fall back on traditional methods of severing their heads from the bodies, wooden stakes through their hearts, or expose them to direct sunlight."

"This is absurd," said the Colonel.

"I know it sounds that way, Colonel, but the evidence supports the possibility of the creatures being real. We have our orders. This is the plan that I have developed. If anyone has any better idea...now is the time to tell me."

No one spoke.

"To summarize the plan, at 1200 today, the first team of six goes in and attempts to place the collars on the creatures. A second team of six, prepared to spray the elixir, or hack off the heads, will back them up. The third team is prepared to blow the place as a last resort. If all goes well, we will hold the creatures temporarily in their present location until transport is arranged." Reese looked at Lieutenant Johnson. "It is imperative you choose men that are trustworthy. This is an operation that can never be acknowledged, no matter what happens."

"My men understand that any operation is classified and never to be discussed." Johnson said.

"Good. I will be going with you. Major Barkley will wait outside and control the remote devices. If anything goes wrong after the collars are on, we will communicate to him to inject the mixture. Any other questions?"

"Suppose that all of this works," said Colonel Antol. "You get your creatures and all that you think about them is true. Then what? What happens to them?"

"I don't know, sir. I'm just following orders," Reese said, but from the look on the Colonel's face, he knew he didn't believe him.

THE SUN WAS directly overhead. Commander Reese surveyed the teams of men as they made their final preparations for the mission. They were situated about 300 yards from the ruins on a hill that overlooked the area. He saw some looks of bewilderment in their faces with the unfamiliar actions of conducting an operation in broad daylight rather than under the cover of night. He imagined they felt naked in the sunlight. Once they were underground, and in the darkness, he hoped they would relax and be ready for whatever they encountered there.

In a way, one team of men was going against another team of...creatures. The men were highly trained in the use of weapons and hand-to-hand combat. The creatures had years of experience of avoiding traps and detection. They would not leave their sanctuary unprotected without traps. Who would prevail? Had he made enough contingency plans? What contingency plans did the creatures have?

He was unsure if they were making the right decision even though he felt the importance of the mission and the authority he had been given was a vote of confidence. But what was he going on? Myths he had read and studied from old books, wives tales he had heard from local residents. The only solid evidence that supported his theories was the satellite surveillance, and the medical information of the two dead girls. And what of his own personal plans for the chance to study the creatures? How far would he go to achieve that end?

What if these creatures were stronger than they imagined? If they had to enact the fatal last measure, he and the rest of these men would be buried under the rock as the old ruins were blown up. Or these creatures might escape and seek vengeance on the local populace. It was too late now; he was committed and he needed to concentrate on the next move.

The SEALs wore their standard camouflage uniforms, but instead of standard issue military boots, they wore their mountain-climbing shoes because of the uncertainty of the terrain. Each member was wearing a lightweight voice-activated communications headset. At their waists, along with their 9mm pistols, they had been given razor-sharp machetes. Reese was surprised that they were able to get hold of them with such short notice, but then again, he knew SEALs were capable of obtaining whatever weapons were necessary.

Under normal circumstances, they would all wear night goggles. But this time, it would hinder their work once they reached the bodies. The creatures would not give off very much heat now that the blood they had ingested turned cold. Only two members of each team had goggles, just in case anything went wrong and they needed to escape in the darkness. Each member had a powerful red beam light that would be their primary light source once they entered the crypt. The red beam would not interfere with the night goggles' effectiveness.

The SEALs had been divided up into three teams. Team One carried the elixir in a modified canister that sprayed it in force. Team Two carried the collars that would be placed around the necks of the creatures, if all went well. Team Three was assigned the ordinance and final line of defense if anything went wrong.

Team Three reported that their task to setup the explosives was complete. They had set-up their detonator west of the ruins, behind a natural mound of dirt that would offer protection from the blast. Those six men were armed to the hilt, to include a small rocket launcher and enough hand grenades to fend off a small army. Their instructions were explicit; blow up the entire area if given the word or if the two teams did not return prior to the sun touching the horizon.

"Are you ready?" asked Johnson.

Reese shook off his feelings of trepidation. "Yes."

"Are you sure you want to go in there? We can stay in communication with you the entire time."

"No. I have to go with you. But make no mistake, you are in tactical command and I will advise."

"Understood," Johnson answered and stared at Reese with an unnerving cold stare that reflected no emotion—the perfect military visage.

"What is it Lieutenant?"

"How did you ever get involved with this, sir?" Johnson asked in a toneless manner that reflected no disrespect.

"I happen to have the background that someone thought would be valuable. I never thought that we would ever get to this stage."

"Well, here we are." Johnson checked his watch. "It's time to go. I think it would be best if you took position behind me when we go in."

"Sounds good," said Reese. He exhaled deeply.

"One more thing, Commander. These men are my family. I will not allow undue harm to come to them. If things get crazy and there is no way the mission can be accomplished, we'll wipe out the place."

"Understood," Reese said. "Let's do it."

Johnson gave the orders for the men to move in, Team One in the lead and Team Two to follow.

Reese willed his body forward noticing how warm and comforting the sun's rays felt and how he was leaving the light behind...hopefully for only a while.

THE DARKNESS swallowed them up as they proceeded down the stone stairs into the depths of the ruins. Within minutes, only red lights illuminated the cavern. The cool smell of damp stone surrounded them. Moisture oozed from the walls in areas, the red lights reflecting the droplets, giving them the appearance of dripping blood.

"This is a communications check, call it off by the numbers," Johnson's voice came through on the tiny headsets they all wore. Members called out their assigned numbers; Reese waited until the end and responded himself.

"Proceed," Johnson's voice came through. "One and Two have the point."

The point men moved the red beams from the stone walls to the ceiling. The eerie glow unsettled Reese, reinforcing the image that they were covered in blood. The rest of the men moved onward and into the darkness.

They knew that the area under the ruins was expansive, but knew no other specifics. Locals had some information and the historical society had a little more but neither offered any complete picture. Just in case, the last man on Team Two placed tracking sensors on the ground as they proceeded in to ensure they could find their way out and to alert the monitoring team on the outside of their position. Reese found it amazing that something built so long ago could be so complex and that it had survived all the turmoil of this country.

Johnson stopped as communication came in from the point men.

"T intersection," said a voice.

"Left side first," Johnson answered. "Team Two, hold position at T."

"Team Two. Understood," came the response.

As they turned left, it became apparent how easy it would be to get lost down here. Everything looked the same as they followed the passages that wound through the caverns. They came across rooms where the wooden doors had decayed into piles of damp sawdust. Wood that still clung to the iron hinges fell apart at the touch of the disturbed air as they moved through the area.

The air thickened with age as they moved further into the darkness; a musty old smell permeated the air. Reese imagined that the archaic air system that fed the catacombs had failed long ago probably by caving in somewhere at the surface. Simple as it was; when working it was an effective system that drew fresh air in and through the underground and vented somewhere at the surface. But now, the air hung like an old curtain in a movie theater that had never been cleaned and had absorbed the odors of thousands of people who had sat in its presence.

"Hold," the voice came through the headset. "Tunnel ends."

"Back track one and two, we'll wait. Proceed through other corridor."

Within a few minutes, the two Navy SEALs came back and reversed direction down the corridor they had come. Everyone else turned and proceeded in the direction toward the intersection. As they passed Team Two that had taken station at the intersection, glances of acknowledgement were exchanged, but no words.

They proceeded down the opposite tunnel, looking at walls and ceilings that looked the same, the repetitiveness offering its own specter of fear. They passed more of the same, doors of rotting wood that opened into small rooms.

"Hold," the voice called. "Tunnel ends."

"Commander Reese?" Johnson's voice called. "Any suggestions?"

Reese was silent. The vampires had to be here. He had seen them last night on the satellite surveillance. They would hide down here but not in an obvious spot that would be easy to detect. That would be too simple for creatures that had evaded capture and death for hundreds of years.

"The opening to where they are must be concealed is some way to blend in with the walls. There would be a change in the air pressure with that type of enclosure between the two spaces."

"Got it," Johnson answered and then spoke to the point men, "One and two, reverse track and ignite a low light flare. Keep it close to the walls and watch the smoke for any variations in direction or flow."

"Understood." Seconds later, the glowing light from the flare could be seen down the passageway as they proceeded toward where Team One waited. Time seem to stand still as they slowly made their way, holding the flares close to the walls searching for any telltale signs of air escaping to indicate an opening.

Johnson came and sat next to Reese and covered his microphone from his headset as they waited. "What do you think?"

"The room has to be here somewhere," Reese answered.

"Do you think they know we are here?"

"That's a tough call, but from what I understand, during the day when they sleep, they are in a semi-conscious state and somewhat oblivious to what is going on around them. Kind of like a drunk who wakes up but hasn't slept off the full effects of the alcohol. They're awake but only sort of."

"Okay," Johnson said, "but if we don't find anything by time we are to get out of here, then what?"

"I'd blow it up, seal it, and call it a day."

"My thoughts exactly," he said. He left Reese and went from man to man checking their status. There was nothing to do but wait at this point. Then Reese heard the voice over the headset.

"Located," the SEAL said. All the members on Team One looked in the direction of the flare. They saw smoke being pushed by an obvious air current coming through the wall.

"Let's get it open," Johnson said over the headset. Reese felt his stomach tighten.

"Look for a stone that looks out of place," Reese added. "Discolored or worn more than the others. But don't open it until you are..."

It was too late. The SEAL standing on the left side of the door outline, grabbed at a stone and the door swung open with such force that the SEAL standing next to him was hit full force and thrown like a rag doll against the wall. There was an audible cracking sound as bones in his body were shattered by the impact.

The Navy SEALs reacted like a swarm of angry bees as they secured the area around the door, watching for any form of attack. Reese was still shocked at the death he had witnessed.

Once satisfied all was secure, Johnson checked the downed man, but everyone knew he hadn't survived. He felt for a pulse but it was evident that he did not detect any by the look on his face in the red glow of the flare. It became too quiet for Reese as he struggled to find his voice.

"These creatures are very strong and smart. That door is designed to be hard to open, but when it does, between them knowing which side to stand on and their strength, they avoid what just happened and anyone not knowing what to look for, ends up dead."

"Will there be anymore surprises?" Johnson's voice crackled over the headset.

"It's impossible to tell," Reese answered. "Sometimes they have human watchdogs or animals to guard their tombs. But these are...modern-day creatures; there is no telling what they have come up with. All I can say is to approach cautiously."

"Understood," Johnson said. "One and Three, take the point and be careful, use the night vision goggles to look for anything odd that might be a trap. Let's go, we'll pick up Two on the way out." Johnson's voice showed no emotion at the loss of one of his team members, but as with all their discipline, they would not mourn until the remaining team was out of harm's way.

The team entered through the door, feeling the slight change in the air pressure. But there was something else: A hideous smell. Reese compared it to rotting garbage on a hot summer day; a gush of air rose and made him gag. He fought the urge to vomit.

"We're close," Reese said, his voice gasping as he fought to control his stomach.

The doorway led into another narrow passageway that they followed for a few minutes before the point men spoke.

"Large open chamber...four stone crypts on stone pedestals."

"Any movement?" Johnson asked.

"None. All quiet."

"Hold station Team One. Team Two?"

"Team Two," responded a new voice.

"Follow our markers and rendezvous on point position."

"ETA one minute."

Johnson moved toward where Reese waited and again covered his microphone.

"What do you think?"

"We do them one by one," Reese began. But if we can determine which one is the master...or dominant one, that is the one we must try and capture first. Then maybe, the rest will submit."

"You don't sound too confident."

"It's legend. I don't know if it's true," he admitted. "We need to take precautions and be ready to kill them all."

"Agreed." Johnson said, then received a message that Team Two was in position.

"Let's do it," he said. "Team One and Two, move in."

They entered into the open chamber that held the stone crypts. The chamber had a high ceiling of twelve to fourteen feet, the blocks of stone neatly carved into perfect squares that comprised the walls. The stone was covered by a fine layer of dirt and muffled the sounds of their approach.

Johnson indicated for some of his men to take up defensive positions. Reese studied the arrangement of the crypts and noted one of the four sat slightly off center from the other three and decided the leader might be in that one. He gestured to the coffin. Johnson nodded in response.

The plan called for four men to handle the operation: One would open the crypt; the second would stand ready with the spray solution;

the third would place the collar on the creature; the fourth held a poised machete to be used as a last resort. Two men would stand at each crypt with solution and machete if the others awakened before they were ready to handle them. The rest of the men stood at the ready with their pistols.

They approached the first crypt. Reese and Johnson followed the four men who were assigned to open the first crypt. The SEAL assigned to the task of removing the lid, his arms the size of most men's thighs, placed his hands on the sides and tested the weight. He nodded that he could slide it off. Johnson gave him the silent go ahead by nodding. The man slid the off the lid and sent it crashing to the ground, the sound deafening as it slammed onto the ground.

Inside laid the body of a man, about twenty-five years of age, dressed in traditional local garb, and appearing serene in a state of sleep. His skin appeared to be pale, but in the light it was hard to determine the actual shade. All in all, he appeared to be a human, not a monster.

The Team appeared mesmerized by the tranquility of the sleeping man, even Reese momentarily wondered if this sleeping man could be a monster that killed to survive. But when his eyelids began to flutter, as it appeared to ascend to wakefulness, Reese spoke to break the inactivity of the group.

"Keep that spray ready," he barked. "Let's get the collar on...quickly!"

The SEAL with the collar readied it for installation as the creature's eyes opened. He stopped as the red feral eyes stared at him. Time seemed to stand still for all of them as the creature's eyes surveyed the scene around him, registering the situation. Seeing that the sanctity of their crypt area had been violated, the creature became alarmed and prepared for attack as its features hardened and fangs protruded.

Reese knew that if they didn't move now, this creature would attain an advantage and all would be lost. But he found himself paralyzed by the eyes of the creature and was unable to move or speak.

"Give it a short burst of the spray!" Johnson's voice screamed, breaking the trance.

The SEAL with the canister hesitated before the command registered in his mind and then he keyed a short burst at the creature. The molecules of the spray seem to hang in the air, crawling through the space between it and the creature. Finally the elixir touched the creature and tiny rivulets of flame burst along his skin. The creature screamed and writhed in its crypt. Its flesh turned dark as blood oozed from the burned areas.

"Listen to me," Reese said to the creature as its writhing slowed, but had not ceased. "I know you can understand me. We can cover you with this if you do not do as you are instructed. Do you understand?"

A guttural growl emitted from the creature.

"Answer me or die!" Reese shouted. "Stand ready to spray!"

"I under...stand..." the creature said.

"A device will be placed around your neck. Do not attempt to attack the man or remove the device or you will die." Reese gestured for the SEAL who held the collar to come close. The SEAL raised the creature's head, carefully avoided the sharp teeth and quickly attached the device. Reese held a remote in his hand that would control the injection in various amounts into the creature's system.

The creature, now almost totally recovered and healed from the initial spraying, raised his hands to the collar as if meaning to tear it off. Reese's finger was posed over the button; he placed the injection quantity to its lowest level and pressed the button.

The creature violently lurched in the crypt as the mixture made its way into its body. It screamed.

"Do that again and I will kill you," said Reese. "Do anything but what I tell you and you will die a painful death. I think you know that now, don't you?"

The creature settled into its crypt and stared at Reese. It bared its teeth in an act of defiance. Reese posed his finger over the button again.

"I understand," the creature said disdainfully. Its low and regal voice was level and controlled. "What do you want?"

"Listen carefully," said Reese knowing he had the full attention of the creature. "Any move you make is being tracked, both by myself and someone on the outside of this area. Any sudden moves will result in the device at your neck being activated. Understand?"

"Yes, I understand."

"Do you have a name?" Reese asked.

"I am Dimitri." His eyes glowed red in the low light.

"All right, Dimitri. I assume you are the leader of this group?" He indicated the other stone crypts.

"In a way, I am their leader."

"We offer the same arrangement to each one, they either accept the collar or die. Can you speak with them without them leaving their crypts?"

"I can speak to them through their dreams," he answered and then added, "What is it that you want from us?"

"Tell them now that we will kill them if they resist the placement of the collars on their necks. I want them—"

One of the other crypts opened—the top flipped off by the powerful thrust of one of the creatures. He leapt out of his crypt and attacked the two men flanking his crypt. Before anything could be done, one man was down, his throat slashed and gushing blood onto the stone floor; the other was within the grasp of the creature that displayed large nails from his hands and elongated teeth from his mouth.

"No Josip!" Dimitri yelled, but it was too late to stop the bloodshed. Josip sliced the throat of the other man and dropped him onto the stone floor next to the other corpse. The back-up SEAL team, although surprised by the swiftness of the attack, responded as planned. The men with elixir-filled canisters covered the area with the fine spray of mixture before the attack progressed. The creature named Josip howled in pain as his body was covered with rivulets of fire. It collapsed to the ground, screaming, the burning flesh smoldering as he rolled on the ground.

"Quick!" Reese yelled. "Get the collar on him. If he makes a move, douse him and cut off his head." He was surprised at the viciousness of the words coming out of his mouth. Dimitri looked at him with a loathing sneer.

"Will he recover?" Reese asked.

"Possibly," Dimitri answered. "The rest will not pose any problem."

"We'll see."

The collar was placed on the creature and he was returned to the crypt. The men, prepared for a reoccurrence of another attack, guarded the other crypts. Johnson checked the two bodies on the ground, his look conveyed the story; both were dead. But he was prepared to finish what he had come to do. He indicated the next crypt to Reese that was to be opened. Reese nodded.

They removed the lid and found the creature lying there awake and alert but not offering any resistance. Reese made Dimitri move in that direction so that the creature could see that Dimitri wore the collar. The collar went on without any form of resistance except a stare that was cold enough to freeze a man's soul.

When they were done, the creatures were given a small example of how the collar worked and its affect on their bodies. After they had calmed down after the test, Dimitri spoke quietly to the rest and then turned and spoke to Reese.

"What are you going to do with us?"

"That's a good question," Reese said. "For now, you will remain here under guard."

"We need to feed," Dimitri said.

"We will bring a cow down here later. You will not leave this space. If any motion is detected by the sensors we have installed, the collars will be activated."

"I understand."

"Is there anything else you need to...survive?" Reese asked.

"Our freedom," Dimitri said. "How did you find us, and who told you of the elixir?"

"A man." Reese answered. Why he volunteered this information puzzled him; he hadn't even hesitated about responding to Dimitri's question. The answer seemed to flow from him.

"His name?" Dimitri asked.

"Idriz Laupki." *Stop it. Why was he answering his questions?*

Dimitri closed his eyes. After a few moments he looked toward the crypt that held Josip and shook his head.

"No more questions!" said Reese. He shook his head to clear his thoughts. "You pull that hypnotic crap again and you'll be punished. Do you understand?"

Dimitri turned to face Reese. "Punished? It's too late to worry about that now, our punishment has already begun."

CHAPTER 9

COMMANDER SCOTT at SOCOM finished his conversation with Commander Reese and replaced the secure phone in its red cradle on his desk. Instead of taking the report to the General, Scott sat there for a few moments, thinking about the conversation.

He had seen many strange situations in the time of his service under General Stone, but those were contrived or conjured up by man. Here was something truly bizarre, something straight out of a nightmare. These creatures...or vampires as he would call them even though he noted that Reese did not use that term, existed and had been captured.

"Scott," said the General as he entered his office. "Have we heard from Reese yet?"

"Ah...yes sir." Scott's throat felt dry and uncomfortable. "Just called in, they...have them."

General Stone's face lit up as the realization of the words struck. "They have them! We actually have them! This is fantastic!" He yelled like a child whose wildest dream had come true.

"The SEALs lost three men in the capture," Scott added.

"Who would have thought," said Stone, either ignoring the remark or not caring to comment. "These creatures exist and they are ours. "

"They lost three men in the attack," Scott repeated.

"I heard you," Stone answered abruptly. "Let me enjoy this moment will you, Scott? Don't you see? After all this damn time, don't you see the potential? After all the crap that I have had to endure from my colleagues—not being able to take revenge for my daughter. Three lives spent today will save many more in the future."

"Sir?" Scott said confused. "How will that—"

"Never mind." Stone cut him off. "We have to make arrangements. We need a story about the three deaths. Make it a training accident. Maybe a cave-in."

"Yes sir."

"Get with Reese and figure out how we are going to bring the creatures back to the states. They'll be working with the SEALs so let's keep them up Norfolk way, maybe even at Little Creek with the other teams. They'll need quarters...very secure quarters."

"Yes sir."

"I want everyone involved with this to be brought back here for debriefing, and I mean *everyone*."

"The civilian?"

"What civilian?"

"The Serbian, the man who pointed us toward them. His daughters were killed by the creatures."

"I don't like involving civilians in this operation. Make him part of the accident where the three SEALs were killed. I want all loose ends tied up, Commander."

"I understand sir, but he is the one that developed the elixir, the solution that keeps the creatures controllable. We have not learned how to duplicate it yet."

"Bring him back then. But I want the liquid studied and its contents determined. After that, get rid of him."

"Understood," answered Scott.

"Find out who I need to kiss ass or stomp on in order to do this discreetly. Make it look like these are rewards for their efforts in Kosovo."

"Are you going to talk with the Joint Chiefs?"

"Not yet. I want to inspect the creatures and measure their potential."

"Potential?"

"Yes...potential. If we can control them...we will be able to conduct a new campaign of operations and make military history."

"Sir?"

"Christ, you still don't you see it! Get you head out of my ass and everyone else's! There is more happening here than just your own career! Look at what their talents are: They're fast, ferocious, hard to detect, extremely difficult to kill...they're perfect."

"But, they kill for the blood. They're unholy."

"A minor drawback for what they may be able to deliver for us," Stone said with a casual wave of the hand.

"This is extremely risky General, if anyone finds out—"

"That's your job—to make sure no one finds out," Stone said placing his finger on Scott's chest as he smiled at the Navy Commander. "That you should be good at, after all your career is at stake isn't it?" He turned away from Scott. "We will make history," he continued, "but it's the kind of history that no one must ever know about. Do you understand me?"

"Perfectly, sir."

"Now start working on the plans to get them back to the States."

"Immediately, sir."

"One more thing," said Stone.

"Sir?"

"Make sure you let Reese know, if the situation gets out of control, subdue the creatures but do not kill them under any circumstances."

"But what if they should try and escape or kill—"

"Is your hearing not working?"

"It's working fine, sir," Scott answered, his voice shaky. "I'll take care of it."

COMMANDER REESE and Lieutenant Johnson watched the remote viewers that showed their captors in their underground prison. When they had returned from the cavern, Reese felt his knees weaken and had to lean up against one of the stone pillars to keep from falling down. The legends were true, he told himself over and over again. *Vampires actually existed!*

But his energy and excitement were overshadowed at the thought of what his dream had cost so far: the lives of three men. He fought his feelings of guilt over his personal gain, but found those overridden by the General's desire to have the creatures. He only hoped that the men had not died in vain and whatever the General hoped to use the creatures for would outweigh the losses. But what had the General planned? Reese had his suspicions, but he wanted to wait—to study the creatures and to fulfill his lifelong dream.

Johnson finalized the security arrangements for their captors, then made arrangements to have the three bodies removed and taken to the medical facility at the Base Camp. He handled the procedure with a coolness that reflected almost robot-like effectiveness, but Reese imagined that privately, Johnson would deal with his own grief in his own way.

"I'm sorry about the men," Reese said to Johnson.

"So am I," Johnson said looking at him. "They knew the risks. It doesn't make it any easier but it's all part of the life we lead." His gaze returned toward the view screen. "I just hope their sacrifices are worth it."

"General Stone thinks so," said Reese and fell silent as he gazed at the creatures. They had not attempted to remove the collars, but they stared intently at each other, as if studying the devices for points of vulnerability.

"I think we have everything covered for the moment," Johnson said. "We have men outside the room they are in, directly outside of the entrance to the ruins, and one team here in standby."

"I'd feel better if we didn't have distance limitations on those collars," Reese said. "Once we get back to the states, the first priority will be to increase the distance parameters."

"When are we leaving?" Johnson asked.

"As soon as you make the arrangements," Reese said smiling.

"Another challenge," he said. "I live for them, you know."

"It appears that we will be under special assignment for however long they want us. Everyone—and I mean everyone—involved is to head back to Norfolk. So we're going to need a plane with lots of room."

"Not a problem," Johnson said. "We have a C-5 at our disposal at all times."

"Make up a plan, but keep in mind that we have to do everything under the cover of darkness for the special cargo."

"Understood." Johnson answered. "I'll get to work on it right now."

Someone knocked at the door.

"Yes," Reese called. The door opened and it was Corporal Brosnev, the interpreter.

"Sorry to bother you, Commander, but Idriz would like to talk with you."

Reese wondered what he was going to tell the man whose children had been killed by the creatures he held captive with orders to not kill them. "Bring him in."

Moments later, they came in. The man's eyes looked intense as they surveyed the room and its occupants. He spoke quickly to the Corporal.

"He says that his mixture worked or you would not be alive. He asks that you please describe how the murderers of his children died a horrible death at your hands."

"His mixture worked just as he said it would. We are very grateful for his help," Reese said, paused and indicated for the Corporal to translate it as he thought about how to explain that the creatures were not dead.

"The creatures are still alive, but they are our prisoners," Reese said and again indicated for the translator to tell him. As the translator told him, the expression on Idriz's features became sharp and drawn.

"We are taking them back to the United States for further study and then...and then they shall be killed," Reese said, knowing the lie was necessary. He didn't like telling the lie; poor Idriz had suffered enough for one lifetime. But there was an opportunity here for research that could not be lost. Reese knew he would not be able to convince Idriz of that now, but maybe later.

Within seconds of translating, Idriz unleashed a volley of words upon them.

"He says, that this cannot be true! His precious daughters are dead because of them. They are beasts of the night that cannot be caged like wild dogs, for they are cunning and will learn how to escape. They must be killed immediately before they murder again."

"They are not going anywhere," Reese said as he showed Idriz the video monitor and continued to speak as the interpreter translated what he said. "You see the band on their necks? That is a special device that contains your elixir." Idriz bent closer to the screen to look. "If they do anything that looks like they might try and escape, the device will inject the elixir into their body."

Idriz continued to stare at the screen with interest without saying anything, but his face portrayed a loathing that was clearly evident.

"They will spend what is left of their lives as our prisoners and will never kill another innocent person." Reese paused, looking for any kind of reaction from the man. He knew there was nothing he could say that would heal his pain at the loss of his daughters—and grief could make him a dangerous man. But there were still things Reese wanted and needed from this man, but he knew that if he told Idriz the truth, that he didn't have a choice in coming back to the States, as were the orders of the General, he might pose a problem.

"They will need a keeper or jailer to watch over them," Reese continued. "And I still need help in learning about what else you know about their pasts. If you wish, you may come with us and help us. We need your help, Idriz."

Idriz suddenly spoke, but not taking his eyes from the monitor. The Corporal translated, "He says that he will come with you to the United States. He won't be their keeper, but their reminder of the painful death that awaits them at his hands."

Reese looked toward Johnson who had been quiet during the exchange, his eyes reflected the same feeling that he had, that Idriz would have to be watched closely.

"SO, YOU ARE awake," Dimitri said to Josip as he sat up from his crypt. Most of the burn marks that he had suffered had healed and only slight blemishes remained. He touched the tight fitting device at his neck.

"Don't touch that! Unless you want more of the poison that burned you."

"What has happened?" Josip asked as he looked around. "Did you kill them?"

"No. There was no way to attack without being killed. Your foolishness almost cost you your life. The device at your neck contains the mixture that killed Franjo. The man, Idriz, whose daughters you killed in your moment of revenge still hounds us."

"How can that be?"

"I don't know. He has gotten help from the Americans and now we are their prisoners."

"Remove the collars," he said as he raised his hands to his throat again.

"Are you not listening? Touch it and you die," Dimitri said. "It has some kind of anti-tampering device built into it. And they are watching us," he said as he indicated the camera mounted into the ceiling. "They also have motion detectors attached to us, they know our every movement. Whoever planned this knows about our kind. How we live, how we sleep. Everything."

"What are they going to do with us?" Josip asked.

"I don't know. The one in charge has not said anything yet."

"We must escape."

"You surely cannot be that ignorant," Dimitri said raising his voice. The others of the group looked toward them now. "Your actions are what brought them down upon us. You will do nothing! We must observe them first and look for their weaknesses and when I feel it is time, we will do what I decide."

Josip remained silent.

"If they were going to kill us they would have done so by now," Dimitri continued, this time speaking to the group. "So they have some other plan for us. We will go along with what they ask. The spirit of cooperation will lower their guard and we will discover our way to escape. Is that understood?"

They all nodded in agreement, Josip last, his hesitation earning him a glare from Dimitri.

The sound of footsteps accompanied with the clop-clop of cow feet down the narrow passageway broke their conversation. The lone cow entered their chambers followed by several men, all heavily armed. The leader of the group stepped forward, the one that they called Commander Reese. Dimitri saw that the one called Idriz was with him.

"Dimitri, I need some information from you about your feeding habits. How long can you go between feeding?"

"You don't want your prisoners to die?"

"Something like that," Reese answered sounding somewhat impatient and not willing to spar in conversation. "We will leave this place in less than a day, and there will be no available food sources for you and your men."

Dimitri looked at the cow that they had brought down. "We will be able to survive for two to three days if we feed on this animal."

"Good," Reese replied. "How about being on an airplane? Does that pose any problems?"

"We...have never been on an airplane before. We have seen them in the sky at night."

"So you don't know if there will be any adverse effects?"

"No. But I don't think it will pose any problems as long as darkness is maintained," Dimitri ventured. "We will need these crypts or something similar."

"I'll take that for a yes about flying. We will bring these," he said indicating the crypts. "We will be back to get you at next sunset," Reese said as he turned to leave.

"Where are we going?" Dimitri asked, then added, "If I may be permitted to know."

Suddenly Idriz spoke, his words echoing in the cavernous area. He had been standing there, along with Corporal Brosnev who had been translating for him during the exchange between Dimitri and Commander Reese. The look on his face and the tone in which he spoke gave the direction of his words.

Josip turned toward him and stared for a few moments and then answered him in their native Slavic tongue.

"What did they say Corporal?" Reese asked.

"When Dimitri asked where they were going, Idriz told the one called Josip that they were going to their deaths."

"And the creatures response?"

"He agreed, but said that they would have much company on their journey."

Reese pondered the remarks for a few seconds then turned back to

Dimitri.

"To the United States," Reese said. "We are going to the United States and I will see any man or creature killed that interferes with our plans." Reese stared at the humans and the creatures, then left.

AS THE NEXT sunset arrived, a wave of activity at the ruins commenced. First the crypts were brought out of the caverns and loaded within standard twenty-foot shipping containers that were on four trucks that awaited them.

Dimitri and his men waited in the now emptied area. Each of them had been given a box for personal belongings. Dimitri busied himself by picking some books from the library. He had so many favorites he was unsure what to take.

"We leave our home," Josip said breaking the silence. "For more than a hundred years this has been our place within our country."

"We do not have a choice in the matter, but what of it?" Dimitri asked "Is not one place like another in a strange way? Besides, were you not saying that you were getting bored?"

"But this is not of our volition and we shall not be free."

"Stop complaining. You are like an old woman at times," Dimitri countered. "Remember what I said: Watch and learn. We will find our freedom in the new land. In America, there are no wars, no constant battering of the countryside by forces. They have large cities with many people who—"

The sound of footsteps approaching interrupted their conversation. Commander Reese and Lieutenant Johnson entered their room.

"Are you ready?" Reese asked.

"We are," Dimitri responded as he tossed a handful of books into his bag.

"Before we go," Reese began, "let me reassure you and your men that every precaution has been taken to prevent your escape or from your attack. When we leave here, each of you will be placed inside a steel container that has your crypt inside of it. That is where you shall remain for the next twelve hours. There are video cameras inside to monitor your movements. Any attempt to leave the container shall result in the activation of the devices at your necks. Each container will be guarded by two men."

"We will be no problem," Dimitri said as other men arrived carrying weapons, spraying devices, and shiny machetes attached to their belts.

"You will be escorted out one at a time."

"We have not met you formally," Dimitri said looking toward Johnson.

"This is Lieutenant Johnson, he is in charge of the men, the Navy SEALs who will be escorting and guarding you."

"Our captor and keeper," Dimitri said bowing his head slightly. "Thank you, Commander Reese for the introduction." Dimitri said. "I sense that we will be spending much time together in the future, I thought it appropriate that we be introduced." Johnson stared coldly at the creature with his usual emotionless features while Reese stared cautiously at Dimitri; he had much to learn about these creatures, but he also remembered from his studies that they could be supreme users of the art of conversation as a distraction to their ulterior motives. There would be time later to develop some kind of understanding to further his studies. There was so much that he wanted to know about their pasts, but now they had to leave.

"Enough pleasantries for now. Johnson, get them moving."

Johnson issued orders to his men. Each one was escorted out into the cool night air and placed inside the shipping container. Dimitri came last and glanced skyward at the night sky, carefully noting the constellations for what may be his last time from his country. In his thoughts, he said his farewell to his teacher and master, Alexander.

Good-bye old friend, we travel to whatever fate awaits us in the land they call America. But I have not forgotten your teachings or the search for the ultimate truth in our existence.

The steel door of the shipping container closed and the trucks drove off into the night.

The loading of the aircraft went as planned and within an hour they lifted off from the runway in Skopje, Macedonia and headed for Norfolk, Virginia. All cargo and passengers were safely tucked onboard the massive aircraft with continual monitoring of the containers that held the creatures.

Every person that had been involved in the operation was on the plane. Reese wondered what the debriefing would consist of, and although not an operator, suspected it was more of a security concern than an informational exchange.

The creatures, showing no adverse effects of flight, settled in their containers in a very human way. The containers were supplied with battery-powered lights in order that cameras could maintain surveillance. Reese was amused and somewhat surprised as he observed them become absorbed in whatever reading material they had brought with them; just as any normal person would do, he thought. So much to learn. So much to understand. Reese decided to try to rest. Their flight would be approximately twelve hours and with the time change, they should arrive under cover of darkness for transference to their new quarters that had been arranged by SOCOM on the Little Creek Naval Base.

But instead of sleeping, he found himself contemplating all that had been accomplished in the past seventy-two hours since his arrival. It amazed him how relatively smooth everything had gone, with the exception of the three deaths. He had already seen the press release of the dead SEALs because Johnson had worked with SOCOM on the verbiage. Personal notifications to the next of kin completed; it was downplayed as a regrettable training accident. There would be an investigation, but it would be under the cognizance of SOCOM so the results would be assured in the end. Reese was saddened that the families would never know the truth of their deaths.

Having the resources and commitment of in-country resources had made it all work. It made him reflect what authority could do in the military without having to answer to the constant oversight of various other organizations as long as everything went okay and the information was contained as it had been in this case. SOCOM was a dark command that did not fall under the constraints that the other geographical commanders did, they hid behind the curtain of national security and other convenient methods similar to those used by the CIA.

"Mind some company?" Johnson asked. He stood in the aircraft aisle, his physical appearance similar to Reese's. He looked tired, but was unable to sleep.

"Sure," Reese answered as Johnson slipped into the seat next to him.

"It's going smooth so far."

"Yes, surprisingly enough." The two men fell into a brooding silence of unasked questions.

"What is going to happen to the creatures?" asked Johnson.

"We get back to Norfolk and find out."

"What do *you* think is going to happen?"

"I...I'm not actually sure," said Reese.

"Not sure or can't say?"

"Don't know."

"No ideas at all?" Johnson asked. "I have some. You want to hear?"

"Sure," Reese said, although inside he really did not want to for fear of resurrecting his own doubts.

"These creatures...are suppose to possess some interesting characteristics that would be of interest to the military. Don't you think?"

"Sure, if the legends are true," admitted Reese.

"Suppose for a minute, they are true."

"All right. Go ahead."

"Number one: We study the physical makeup to determine what makes them work and ascertain if those factors can be duplicated."

"Sounds logical."

"Number two: Destroy the creatures before they can do any harm. Or at least that is what I would hope."

"Keep going." Reese felt the inevitable option coming that he suspected was the true purpose of capturing the creatures.

"Number three: Examine the possibility of using the creatures to perform in a certain way as to benefit us."

"Have them do the dirty work, you mean?"

"Something like that," Johnson said. "The ultimate killing machines as long as you keep them fed...and why not let them feed on the victims?"

"Kill two birds with one stone," Reese added but quickly regretted his analogy. "All of this is purely speculative thinking on our part, right?"

"Of course," Johnson said.

"Don't you think that there would be a particular morality issue with this line of thought?"

"Morality? Who says that the military needs morality? Not me. Changing times call for unique actions. Bottom line is to get the job done and everything...everything is expendable when it comes to that. Besides, think about it from a military standpoint. Would you mess with a country that had control of creatures like these?"

"Good point, but if another country knew, then it might become known to the public."

"I don't think so," Johnson began. "Could you see our military claiming that some vampires from Russia or something attacked us? Hard to swallow and no flag officer in his right mind would ever make that claim if he wanted to remain on active duty."

Reese exhaled. "You realize what we are talking about will never be known outside of a very exclusive group?"

"Sure," Johnson said following Reese's line. "It would all appear as if no one could be involved in something as crazy as all this. Sounds like we are writing some science fiction story, huh?"

"Yeah," Reese said. "Some crazy stuff, but you know what?"

"What?"

"Who the hell would have ever thought that the damn creatures ever existed?"

"Who says they exist, Commander?"

Reese stared at him searching for the meaning to his statement.

"After the debriefing," Johnson began, "I have a feeling that they won't. In fact I would be willing to bet that the entire mission never happened."

Johnson looked at Reese with his usual emotionless expression that indicated the subject was closed. "We should try and get some sleep while we can," Johnson said. He laid back in his seat and closed his eyes.

Reese stared at him before he reclined in his own seat. He thought of General Stone and wondered about the note again. His capture of the creatures made him a direct part of whatever happened and from this point on if they were used as Johnson had suggested, he would be as...guilty as the creatures themselves.

Johnson stirred from his supposed rest and turned toward Reese.

"Sweet dreams, Commander," he said.

CHAPTER 10

COMMANDER SCOTT arrived on the quarterdeck of the Naval Special Warfare Group Two Building on the Naval Amphibious Base in Virginia Beach, Virginia; the largest base of its kind and the major operating station for the amphibious forces of the United States Atlantic Fleet.

The facility, comprised of more than nine thousand acres that includes four locations in three states, was home to thirty ships. The base itself contains seventy-five tenant commands that reside on the property; some of were supporting units while others were operational and dealt with amphibious operations. One of the tenants, the Commander Naval Special Warfare Group Two, was comprised of the Coastal Patrol Craft, Special Boat Units, and the Navy SEAL Teams.

Commander Scott was escorted into the Group Two Commander's office. Navy Captain John Foster impatiently awaited his arrival at this early hour of the morning.

Foster was a lean and tall man, forty-eight years of age, and destined to never make Admiral, at least that is what the General said. But Scott was ordered to not indicate that in any way: The General needed Foster to make the preparations and if things went bad, Captain Foster could be used as a patsy to take the blame as the General shored up his position.

"Captain Foster," Scott said as he extended his hand.

"Commander Scott, welcome to Little Creek. Please have a seat."

Scott sat in the plush leather chair opposite the Captain's desk.

"Commander I have to admit the General has had us jumping through some big hoops in the past forty-eight hours."

Scott detected the anxiety in the man's voice. The General had made some big demands on short notice. "Yes sir, I apologize for the General. I can assure you that it is of the utmost importance."

"There's a new line I haven't heard before. Whenever someone needs something done in a hurry, they throw buzz words out at you that don't mean a damn thing."

"Captain, I'm sure the General—"

"We have just about everything ready. Now tell me what this is all about."

"Sir, we appreciate your efforts, but at the moment, until the General gives the green light, I can't say anything more than what you have already been told."

"I like to say I understand, Commander, but I have a right to know what is going on."

"Yes sir, but please understand my position—"

"The hell with it," the Captain scoffed. "I know you have your orders. I hope the General has a good memory when my name comes up before the board for Admiral. I'm sure he may have some influence there."

"I know the General thinks highly of you sir, that is why he knew he could call on you for this important task."

"I'll take that for a yes."

"Yes sir...and thank you," said Scott, relieved.

"Here's what we have." Foster stood and walked to a large wall map of the base. "We have selected an old building that is not in use at the far end of the base." He pointed to a red square marked on the map. "It only has one road for access and if you're not going to the building you have no reason to be on it so it's easy to guard. The building is old but still in good shape, built in 1945 when the base was commissioned. It has three-foot thick cinderblock walls, no windows, and a roof made of the largest timbers I have ever seen.

"Dimension wise it has about seven thousand square feet, plenty of room for what you need. High-security doors have been installed and monitoring cameras have been put throughout the building and are controlled from a main control room. The natural layout of the interior is about evenly divided into living and working spaces and has been furnished. A high security fence, electrified and wired at the top, has also been installed. It circles the entire circumference of the area."

"How about visibility from a distance?" Scott asked.

"Blocked by the woods. You would never know the place is there."

"Great." Scott was pleased with how everything was shaping up so far. "What about the other building requirement?"

"You weren't serious about that were you? About the stable and barn?"

"Ah...yes sir. We were." Scott lost his good feeling.

"I thought you were kidding about that, like the old expression...you know, when someone asks for a lot they usually end up with the 'you may as well throw in the barn with it while you're at it.' You have heard that expression before, haven't you?"

"No sir."

"You've been with the General too much, lost your sense of humor." He paused as he saw the expression of worry on Scott's face. "Relax, Commander, as fate would have it, the other reason why we chose this area was because that was where they had the horse stables on base. They're on the backside of the building. They've been empty for years, but we repaired the major problems and are finishing up some minor repairs. We'll have it ready by this evening."

The color returned to Scott's face as he breathed a sigh of relief. "Just one last thing before we go out and take a look. How about the cattle?"

"There are a half dozen cows out there now. You wouldn't believe what I had to go through to get them," he said, exasperated. "Can you see me trying to write a justification to purchase cattle? I'm not even going to tell you where I got them from...I'll be damned if I'm going to jail for buying damn cattle. What the hell are you guys going to do anyway, have one hell of a cookout?"

"Not exactly sir, but if they do, you can be sure you will be invited," Scott said trying to add a little humor to his tone.

"I'd better be after all I have gone through," Foster said as he picked up the keys for the vehicle. "Let's go and take a look." He took steps toward the door and stopped to look at the Commander. "I won't forget, you know, about the barbecue. Probably going to be a lot of VIPs there. Wouldn't hurt my career to meet some of them."

Scott didn't say anything as the Captain marched out of the room. *This is one barbecue you don't want to go to, Captain, unless you want to be the meal.*

THE VEHICLES moved smoothly from the runway at the Norfolk Naval Air Station toward the Naval Amphibious Base Little Creek located less than thirty minutes away in the pre-dawn morning. Their convoy of three semi-trucks and six other associated vehicles would not attract any undue attention in the largest Naval community in the world. There was always an exercise going on, or ship battle groups coming and going at all hours of the night at anytime during the year.

As they approached the main gate to the base, Reese noticed Commander Scott from SOCOM waiting at the gate with the sentries. As the vehicle stopped, he jumped in along side Reese.

"Welcome back," he said in an all too cheery voice that grated on

Reese's tired disposition. "And congratulations on one hell of a job. The General is extremely pleased."

"Thanks," Reese responded but without enthusiasm. "Is he here?"

"Not yet, but he should be in a day or so."

"That's good. All of the men are worn out." Reese said as he rubbed his eyes.

"All the quarters are ready. The living quarters for all of you are within the same facility as the...new team."

"We're going to be living there, too?" Reese asked, surprised. "I have my own quarters in Norfolk."

"The General thought it imperative that the group be kept together for a while longer," Scott said.

"How long is 'a while'?" asked Reese.

"Until the General says it is. You can discuss that with him if you like."

Reese sat in silence for a few seconds before he spoke again. "What did you call them? The new team?"

"Yes. We had to call it something in order to classify the expenditures under the black operations account."

"Black operations," he repeated and found it amusing. "We should call them Team of Darkness. It would be appropriate in more ways than one."

"I like that," Scott said. "Kind of a catchy title. You can bet an eyebrow or two will go up with that one. The General loves to keep people guessing."

"How far to the secure area?" Reese asked wanting to change the subject.

"Not much further. I took a look at it today and was quite impressed."

"What about security? Men to guard and monitor our new arrivals?"

"Lieutenant Johnson and his team have been permanently assigned to this operation."

"He's a good man, but a little too military for me." Reese commented. "But his men performed well. It was a shame that we lost three."

"Yes, it was," Scott said. An uncomfortable silence fell between them.

"What about me? Do I go back to my assignment?"

"We need you with this assignment. Your background is pertinent and critical to this mission as is evident by the successful capture."

"I just supplied the information, Johnson handled the operational side. I am interested in these creatures, but I need to know where is this going."

"What do you mean?" Scott said.

"These creatures...what will happen to them?"

"The General will explain all of that when he gets here." Scott said in a well-rehearsed statement. "Here we are."

Reese did not like the way the conversation had been ended—without any answers to his most important questions.

The trucks entered the road that led to the compound. Thick dense woods concealed its location from passing traffic. In a few minutes they arrived at an area encircled by fencing and illuminated by high-intensity lighting. Their small convoy stopped. Reese and Scott got out of the vehicle and were joined by Johnson.

"Commander Scott," Johnson said as he saluted, then shook hands.

"Good work, Lieutenant. I was just explaining to Commander Reese that you and your men have been assigned to compound security and monitoring."

"We better take a look," Johnson said. Another sign of Johnson's devout allegiance, thought Reese. *Ask no questions, just do as you are told.*

Johnson selected various members of his team for immediate assignments and took the rest on a tour of the facility. Reese and Scott followed, Scott explaining the layout. Reese met Johnson in the control room of the facility.

The control room was completely sealed, designed to withstand any type of forced entry. Entry to this door and all of the others in the facility were controlled by electronic card and thumbprint; considered the most secure method in private industry and high-level government. Inside the control room, they became acquainted with the video monitors that displayed every inch of the facility, the security alarms, and the motion detectors. The last piece of equipment to go in was the remote device that would activate the collars on the creatures.

"That about covers it for now," Reese said. "You happy with it, Johnson?"

"Looks good. But the true test is to get our friends out of the containers and turn them loose in their new quarters. The containers are off the trucks and ready to be opened. Double protection is ready."

"Let's get to it," Reese said.

Orders were passed and the men arranged in their hurried

arrangement for double protection. The first team would unload one creature at a time and escort him into the area. The SEALs would be armed with the elixir in their spray apparatuses. At the same time the creatures would be monitored from inside the control room in the event of an attack whereby the collar device would be activated. Reese and Johnson accompanied the first team as they opened the container that carried Dimitri; Commander Scott stood back as if waiting to see some type of show. They unbolted the door and swung it open.

Dimitri stood there, his stance reflecting that of a man that had just disembarked a train. He inhaled the air deeply, seeming to digest and dissect the smell to determine its individual ingredients. He smiled at Reese and Johnson.

"We are near the ocean?"

"Yes," Reese said. "We are at our destination."

"And that is where?" He asked.

"Virginia," Reese stated. "These facilities are to be your home for the immediate future. We must get you and your men into these facilities quickly, dawn is less than a hour away."

"Yes, I can sense it coming. Our sense of timing in regards to the sunrise is acute."

"Let your men know what's happening. Remind them that the same precautions are in place that have always been and that as before, we will not hesitate in using them."

Dimitri looked around, studying the faces of the armed men; he saw the same armaments as before. He raised his hand to the collar at his neck.

"These are very hard on our flesh, perhaps we can have different ones that will not abrade our skin."

"We will discuss that later. I want you and your men inside," ordered Johnson.

"Very well," Dimitri said and closed his eyes for several seconds as he communicated with the rest of his men. Reese was fascinated by this ability and hoped to learn more about it. "They all understand and are ready," said Dimitri.

"Okay. You first," Johnson said as they escorted him into the facility. The area consisted of individual rooms for each creature. The furniture was sparse but appeared comfortable. Each room contained an alcove in which their crypt had been placed. The door to each room was also keyed with magnetic card reader and thumbprint verification.

"It's not much, but we didn't have time. If our plans go okay, we will add some more niceties for you," Reese said.

Dimitri scanned the area but did not speak.

"Did you hear what I said?"

"Yes. We are accustomed to living in an underground environment that had much in terms of amusement. This is quite satisfactory for a prison."

"We have to get everyone inside right now. Can you wait until this evening to feed?" Reese asked, his tone reflecting the obvious disdain at the thought.

"You find the concept difficult to comprehend don't you? The fact that we must take the blood from a living creature in order to survive."

Reese said nothing.

"I have a feeling you will get use to it," Dimitri said. "As I will have to get use to whatever it is that you have in store for us."

Reese still didn't say anything. He turned and exited the creature's quarters ensuring that the door locked shut behind him. He couldn't help but wonder if Dimitri was right.

"They look like normal men," Commander Scott said, surprising Reese out of his thoughts.

"What did you expect?" Reese snapped. "Did you think they would have three eyes or fangs that hung down to their chins?"

Scott was surprised by the outburst as he saw a frightened look in Reese's bloodshot and weary eyes.

"But don't worry, they possess the attributes you and the General are looking for. Turn your back on them for a millisecond and they will slit your throat like you and I open up a can of soda, and then drink it with as much delight."

"Whoa...Reese," Scott said holding up his hands. "Take it easy. I wasn't trying to be funny or anything. To most of us that is the image we conjure up. We don't have the background that you do."

Reese calmed himself. He sensed the edginess had been growing inside of him since the conversation on the plane with Johnson. His own doubts and fatigue plagued him. "Sorry. Didn't mean to jump on you."

"You're tired," said Scott. "Get some rest and we will talk tomorrow."

"Right...right. Tomorrow." Reese said and walked off to finish unloading the remaining three creatures. They were placed into their individual quarters. Job done, Reese decided to call it a night. He headed to the living quarters, meeting Johnson on his way and accompanied him.

"Nice place?" Reese asked.

"Home sweet home Commander." Johnson smiled. Reese imagined that Johnson really liked the place.

"I think Dimitri is right. It's a prison. I'm just not sure who is the prisoner anymore. Them or us?"

CHAPTER 11

"WE ARE CAPTIVES nonetheless, " said Josip as the four of them stood in the main meeting room of their quarters; sunset having arrived after their first sleep in their new surroundings. When they awoke, they found new clothing that had been left for them. They saw this as another step in their loss of their own identities as they were now dressed in the same blue coveralls and black boots.

As usual, Andre and Iliga listened rather than spoke. They were always quiet and sullen, almost withdrawn. More so after they had been changed. Dimitri wondered if this was possibly attributed to their weakened state at the time when Alexander took them. Though they lacked speech in any great amount, their comprehension was fine in that they understood everything and followed Dimitri or Josip without hesitation.

"You must be careful with your words," Dimitri said. "We would not want to appear ungrateful to our hosts," as he indicated the remote cameras in the room. "Your statement is correct, but we must make the best of the situation."

Then, speaking in a tone that the audio equipment could not pick up, but they would because of their enhanced hearing abilities, he said, "Remember what I said earlier. We study and learn before we try anything. We are in a new part of the world that we do not understand. In our many years of our existence we have experienced much, but our country is not like the West. They are different than the back-country peasants that we are use to dealing with for cattle or—"

"Did you smell it?" Josip asked, interrupting Dimitri. "When they opened the doors it was so strong."

"The ocean...yes I smelled it."

"And the other...did you smell that also?   The smell of humans...of the blood of millions in the area?"

"Yes, that too," Dimitri conceded. "Again, it is not like our home. Here the people are much closer and in large quantities. It will require more control of our hunger."

"And our captors will tempt us with their blood as they study us."

Josip said. "Have they revealed anything to you yet?"

"No, but I believe soon we shall learn what they want of us. I will handle the one that appears to be in charge...the one called Reese. He has an interest that I can tap into. He is interested in us as a curiosity, something from the past. The others have something else in mind which we will learn through him."

"They are soldiers as we were once," Josip said with a bit of reminiscence in his voice. "We marched off to protect—"

"And you see where that got us. We lost our human souls to this other side that we call life. For what? The glory of fighting to save our country? And what would it have mattered? Look what has happened over the years in our precious country. It goes from one war to another and now they have even resorted to killing each other. And we are in the middle, between life and death with no will to kill ourselves and our main focus on preserving our lives."

"You would prefer death?" Josip asked.

"No, of course not. But what of...purpose besides our self-preservation?"

"We are creatures, who belong to our own," Josip said. "We survive."

"But for what purpose I ask you again? We have the abilities through our superior life spans and physical attributes—less our few hindrances in the light of day. Our physical surroundings present no problem to us like our human counterparts."

"What do you want, Dimitri?" Josip asked. "We have purpose. We must survive. That is all we will ever have."

"Of course we have all that, but there is more. What if survival was not a problem anymore? If food sources were always available and no one hunted us? We occupy our time with reading and exploring the world around us and remain unattached as much as possible to what goes on around us. I must have more...we must have more," Dimitri said as he turned away from the group.

"You have something on your mind, some grand idea don't you?" Josip asked aloud, this time in a normal tone. He no longer cared if the humans heard him.

"I don't know," Dimitri responded. "Perhaps it will become more clear in time. Maybe it's just the environment change."

"Perhaps if you drank the human blood it would raise your subconscious ideas," Josip said in the lower tone, not to be overheard.

"That's not an option, Josip. Get it out of your head. It will only lead to trouble."

"I will put it aside for the moment," he said. "But I will not forget it. Nor should you."

The comment jolted Dimitri. This was one of the times that Josip was correct although Dimitri would not agree with it as easily as Josip would like. If he were to compare it to anything, drinking human blood was like indulging in a fine whiskey as compared to drinking animal blood that would be like table wine.

Enough! He could no longer think about it. His head pounded. He was hungry, as were the others. He saw the anxiety building in them. He had hoped that Reese had made some kind of arrangements for their feeding cycle.

As if in anticipation of his request, a voice sounded from the monitoring system as a door in the rear area of their quarters buzzed and clicked open. The voice was familiar and Dimitri recognized it as Reese's. He found it odd that it should come when he had thought about it.

"Go through that door. It will lead down a corridor and out into another closed area. There you will find cattle waiting for you. When you are done return to this area. Is that understood?"

Dimitri moved into the direct line of sight and nodded that he understood the instructions. "And then?"

"Then we have things to do. Tests to conduct on you and your men."

Dimitri nodded and headed in the direction his men had gone. *Tests? But who is testing whom? This is a race for knowledge of strengths and weaknesses hidden under the poorly knitted cloth of mankind that has too many holes in it, my friend.*

FROM THE control room, they monitored the feeding habits of the creatures. For those that had not seen it before, they were riveted by the actions of the creatures taking of their meals. Reese, although still having difficulty with the concept, found himself adjusting to it as just another event. He found it interesting that the cattle became subdued so quickly and let them drink their fill.

"Evening," Commander Scott from SOCOM said as he entered. "Or is it morning for you?" He asked Reese. "Your hours must be reversed to match the creatures now that..." He paused mid-sentence as his gazed moved to the monitor and witnessed the creatures feeding. "My God!"

"What's wrong? Everyone has to eat," said Reese. "Including the Team of Darkness, right?" His voice frothed with more sarcasm than he had intended.

"I suppose so," Scott said. "But it's so...disturbing."

"Disturbing is hardly a strong enough word to describe it."

"So what is the schedule for them today?' Scott asked as he looked away from the monitor with obvious relief.

"Today is test day. Major Barkley has a whole battery of tests to run on them, blood and tissue cultures, the whole gambit. We should have some answers in twelve hours or so. Maybe we can get some insight into what they are."

"Good," said Scott. "The General will be here soon to see what we have come up with."

"I wouldn't get your hopes up," Reese said. "I think we will come up with more questions than answers from the tests."

"Why?"

"I don't think there are biological answers. It boils down to a question for theology. I don't know and I don't think anyone else does either."

"Let's wait to see what results they get before we dismiss any physical evidence," Scott replied. "You know the General doesn't like questions...he wants answers."

"What does the General think he has here?"

"That will be for him to tell you, not me. I'm just a messenger."

"I know...I know."

Major Barkley entered in to the control room area carrying what appeared to be a collar device.

"Commanders," he said in greeting. "I'm ready to begin testing when you are. I also have made some adjustments to the collar devices that will give them greater range and they have built-in a tracking device. And if comfort is an issue, I've placed a soft material on the inside."

"We can change collars when you have each one in the medical area." Reese turned toward one of the men at the monitor stations. "Let Lieutenant Johnson know so he can get the men prepared."

"Yes sir," the man said. He picked up an internal phone and made the call.

"How are you doing on the elixir ingredients?" Reese asked Barkley.

"That's the damn weirdest thing," he began. "I've analyzed that stuff three ways to Sunday, but when I put the ingredients together, it's just not the same as what Idriz made."

"That is interesting," Reese said. "But...I know this will sound strange but maybe he put a hex or some kind of spell on it."

"I wouldn't know about that," Barkley said. "But I do know that there is a time factor in the effectiveness of it. From what I can tell, it's effective for maybe seven days or so and that is a swag at best."

"Get Idriz onto making more of it," ordered Scott.

"I asked him and he politely refused until he talks with Commander Reese," Barkley said as he looked at Reese.

"Okay, I'll talk with him."

"They're coming back in," one of the monitor personnel said. "They're in the outer corridor now."

"And Lieutenant Johnson?" Reese asked.

"He is in position and ready."

"Let me talk to him first," Reese said. The man on watch dialed the phone and asked the Lieutenant to stand by as he handed Reese the phone.

"Slight change of plans," Reese said into the phone. "I have to speak with our favorite civilian, Mr. Laupki. Can you handle our friends?"

"No problem," Johnson said. "We're getting good at this stuff."

"Don't get overconfident. That's exactly what they're counting on," Reese said with urgency in his voice. "Make sure your men understand that."

"Got it," Johnson replied.

"Your game," Reese said to Barkley.

"I'm not sure which is worse," Barkley said. "Those creatures or the civilian."

"It's close," Reese said as he left the control room.

REESE FOUND Idriz in the observation room that had a direct view into the chamber that Barkley used for a lab. Corporal Brosnev was next to him; the interpreter had become Idriz's constant companion. They watched Barkley take test samples from Dimitri.

Reese was surprised to hear Idriz speaking simplified English terms.

"Have you mastered the English language already?" Reese asked.

"Oh...sir," the corporal said surprised at Reese's appearance. "No sir, but he is making some progress, he already had picked up some since the peacekeeping force had moved into the area."

"Interesting how none of his English came out before," said Reese.

"Good a-a-a-fter-noon," Idriz said slowly.

"Not quite. Good evening would be more appropriate."

"Good eveee-ning...my name... is Idriz Laupki."

"Very good," Reese said and then turned toward the Corporal. "Translate please."

"Yes sir. I'm ready."

"Major Barkley tells me you won't make any more elixir until you talk to me. So here I am."

Idriz spoke to the interpreter who translated and spoke to Commander Reese. "He says that he wants to be involved with what is going on in there," he said pointing to the room where Barkley as working on the creature.

"Why?" Reese asked, although he knew he had promised the man a role in the confinement of the creatures.

"He wants to talk to the one named Josip."

"Okay." Reese knew the urgency of getting more elixir. "Tell him to make another supply of the elixir and I'll assign him to the guard staff and he can talk with Josip. But only under supervision."

The translator spoke with Idriz and turned toward Reese.

"It's a...done...deal," Idriz said fumbling over the words, then brokered his hand to shake. Reese accepted the hand and shook but did not release it. He spoke to the translator.

"Tell him, that if he tries to do anything that causes the creatures harm, I will have him thrown into a jail cell for the rest of his life. Or better yet, I will throw him in with the damn creatures and let them have a feast on him." Reese paused then continued, "And this time, I want him to write out the instructions so that we can make the elixir."

The Corporal translated and Idriz smiled and nodded in agreement. Reese didn't like the smile and released Idriz's hand.

"Now get to work," Reese said and left the room.

REESE USED his electronic card and pressed his thumb against the reader device; the door opened and he found himself inside of Dimitri's quarters. Another man, one of the Navy SEALs that stood watch outside of the door, accompanied Reese. This followed the two-man rule created for protection when in the presence of the creatures. Dimitri sat in a chair reading a book and looked up as Reese entered.

The sharpness of the creature's gaze disturbed Reese, he felt as if the creature could see right through him and knew what he was thinking.

"Ah, the jailer comes at last," Dimitri said as he placed a bookmark inside the book. "Come to see the latest device they have placed around our necks?" He asked as he indicated the new collar around his neck.

"It's time to begin our talks," Reese said trying to maintain a sense of calmness in his voice. "I want to learn about you and your men."

"You really mean, *our kind*, don't you?"

"Yes."

"Please, have seat," Dimitri said and indicated the empty chair across from him. Reese sat, unable to take his eyes of Dimitri. There was an aura that surrounded the creature, radiating a sense of calmness in him that was almost disturbing.

"We adjust quickly," Dimitri said interrupting Reese's thoughts. "We have learned to adapt to changing situations."

"So I see," Reese said. "Can you tell me about you and your men?"

"Why do you want to know of us?"

"I have my reasons."

"A vendetta, isn't it? You wish to get even with someone?"

"No!" Reese said, feeling sweat forming at his brow.

"You know, we can tell if someone is lying," Dimitri said, a small thin smile appearing on his lips. "We can sense the change in the blood, we can hear your heart speed up."

"It's not against one person," Reese said exhaling strongly. "It's against all of them. They all thought I wasted my time chasing the myths of ancient times."

"Why would someone be interested in creatures like myself?"

"I want to know...what happens to your mind over the years. Do you get bored with life and just live to feed to survive to the next day? Or do you have hopes and dreams for the future like everyone else? How does someone occupy eternity?"

"Everything has a purpose in this world, otherwise there would be no reason for existence," Dimitri said although it was not so much to Reese as it was a reiteration of a lesson that Alexander had given him. "Everything must find its place within the fold and creases of life, otherwise it may be squashed out of existence." The image of Alexander left Dimitri's mind. "So many questions, Commander. And now you have the answers right at your fingertips, is that it?"

"Yes."

"Will you tell me why we are here?" asked Dimitri.

"I can tell you what I know," said Reese. "But I do not make the ultimate decision about what happens."

"But you appear to be in charge."

"I am what you would call, a subject-matter expert. I have done my major contribution, capturing you and bringing you here. My main interest has always been the study of ancient histories to include myths and folklore. That is why I am here."

"A further quest for knowledge," Dimitri asked, his eyebrows raised.

"That is my personal desire, yes. But I am in the military, too so it is a double-edged sword you might say."

"I understand. What do you want to know?"

"Tell me about you and your men. Where are you from, how old are you and how did you become a...creature or is vampire the correct term?"

"There were five us," said Dimitri, without addressing Reese's question about vampires. "We were all born around 1890 in a little village not far from the town of Kacanik. Josip and I were best friends and we attracted three others that formed our little group. There was Franjo, who is dead now, and Andre and Iliga."

"They don't speak very much, do they?"

"No. But they understand perfectly. I believe that when we were made, they had been too badly injured by the Germans and Alexander could not save them in their entirety."

"Alexander was the master?"

"Yes. It was around 1915, when the Germans invaded Serbia. We were young and foolish and marched off to fight them. Not quite soldiers but what we lacked in training, our egos made up for, which is a dangerous and stupid combination. The Germans captured us, and tortured us for information we did not possess, but the German Lieutenant used the pretense for obtaining information to carry out his own quest for vengeance. They would have finished us off if not for Alexander saving us. He took us back to his underground sanctuary and then...made us. It was that or death and we chose to live."

"Is the process what is recorded in most myths? The sharing of the blood of the vampire?"

"Yes. There is more to it but that is basically correct. There is no way to reproduce without that process occurring."

"What happened to Alexander?" Reese asked.

"He was killed by an explosive weapon in 1941. The Germans again—as they took our country."

"There was no way to save him?" Reese asked.

"No. The explosive device dismembered him too badly for his

restorative abilities to compensate."

"I'm sorry," Reese said seeing the sadness on Dimitri's face.

"He was a good man," said Dimitri. "He taught us how to survive and how to fight the temptation of human blood."

"Why? I thought—"

"Of course you did," Dimitri said before Reese could finish. "More of your myth and folklore. They say we steal the blood of babies, don't they? I suppose some of it is true, but we can live on the blood of animals just as well as we can on the blood that runs through your body."

Reese winced at the analogy.

"I apologize for the terminology. I am trying to explain the best way so that you will understand."

Reese nodded.

"It is easy to become addicted to the human blood because of the effects, it's like a narcotic. It enhances our thinking and creativity processes." Dimitri paused before continuing. "Don't you want to know?"

"What?"

"If I have drank human blood?"

"Have you?"

"Yes." Dimitri said calmly. "On occasion we would encounter some of the lesser quality of people that the town had discarded such as drunks and vagabonds. If their own kind saw no worth in them, what would it matter if we took them? It was as if the town had given them to us as if to say, take them and save the world from any further foolishness or abuse of such idiots."

"But that was not the case with Idriz's daughters, was it?" asked Reese.

Dimitri eyed Reese with a cautious look. "That was a blood feud that was carried too far. Idriz's parents were makers of the elixir; they used it to keep us away from their cattle. When they did, we stayed away until things got quiet. Then we moved back in and stole some of their cattle for our food supply. This type of arrangement had been going on for years, passed through the generations. We avoided all other unnecessary contact with the villagers."

"So what happened?"

"Idriz's parents came to where we live in the mountains and Franjo found them before we did. He went crazy at the sight of them and killed them both before I could stop him. Idriz sought retribution and arranged a very purposeful trap that snared Franjo. He used a cow that he had continually fed the elixir to until the animal's blood became saturated with it. Franjo drained the animal and ingested the elixir. He died a horrible death. Josip swore to seek revenge, and I told him he could have it, but I never thought that he would take the daughters."

"But he did," said Reese.

"Yes," Dimitri said as he rubbed his face. "I put the issue to the back of my mind. We all agreed to wait and came up with a better way to get food. We decided that in order to avoid a reoccurrence of the missing cattle, we bought cattle from the villagers every few years and drove them up into the mountains. That way they all would believe that Idriz had killed the creature that lurked in the mountains."

"And did it work?"

"Yes. Things had been going well until Josip killed the girls. We had been content in a way to continue our lives hidden in the mountains. One thing about finding yourself immortal is you have anew perspective on all things. There is no more rush or hurry to do or see things. It is just a matter of catering to your fantasies in ways that most men could never dream of." Dimitri looked away and reflected on his words. He turned back to Reese and said, "Now what can you tell me about our future?"

"You're not a fool, Dimitri. You're intelligent, you must know what people are thinking in regards to the powers that you possess and how they might benefit in a military use."

"Of course, the thoughts crossed our minds many times. You know what my country has gone through. It has always been in a constant state of bloodshed. But we do not get involved with the trivial matters of mankind anymore. As I stated earlier, we have a different perspective about the world around us."

"I don't think you will have a choice in that anymore. If your powers cannot be reproduced, you may be—"

"Asked to do things in order to keep on living."

"Yes."

"You are not any fool, either," said Dimitri. "You must surely realize that no good can come from it."

"I know. But I don't have a choice and neither do you."

"There are always choices, Commander Reese. No one knows that better than I do. It's what we do with them that defines our existence."

CHAPTER 12

GENERAL STONE arrived early and without notice, a habit that he enjoyed. He liked catching people off guard; it gave him an advantage that he had found useful on more than one occasion. He especially found pleasure in that it didn't let the ass kissers and brown nosers get ready for him, and there were so many of them these days.

He was no fool and realized that a certain amount of brown-nosing was required, he had done his share on the way up. He mused about how it was so closely related to the Italian Mafia and the skillful art of performing favors in order to have the ability to call in your own one day. He had managed to perform his favors carefully, used those paybacks to rise through the ranks by obtaining the jobs he required in the places that would reap him the most benefits.

He had called in a lot of favors during this latest operation in order to cover his tracks. He may have been in charge of one of the most powerful commands in the world, but it still required him to go outside his chain of command and that was where the danger lay. Most of his favors had come from his buddy, General Arthur Sorrell, who was in charge of the European Command responsible for the operation in Kosovo. Fortunately Arthur had had some rough times in the past where he had been helped out of some very damaging situations from his good friend, Stone. Now they were even and there would be no more help that might jeopardize Arthur's career. The debt had been paid in full.

As he left his rented vehicle that he had picked up at the commercial airport and approached the main entrance door to the facility, he removed the plastic card that Commander Scott had sent him. He placed it in the slot and touched the pad with his thumb to authenticate himself to the security system. The door unlocked with a heavy metallic click, and he went inside as the first strokes of sunrise painted their red-orange glow across the horizon.

He knew the layout having familiarized himself with the plans that Scott had sent. He made his way to the control room where again he used his card and thumbprint and entered into the secure area. He surprised a young Navy SEAL Petty officer who had been looking at the remote camera monitors and making annotations in his desk log. At the sight of the General, the young sailor leaped from his seat as his eyes fixed upon the three shiny stars on the large man's shoulders.

"Sir," the sailor yelled.

"At ease young man," the General said. "I'm early and just poking around some getting a look at the place." The General glanced at the clock on the wall; the time was 0615 in the morning. "I would have liked to have gotten here when it was still night so I could have gotten a look at our visitors."

"We have all of it on tape," the young sailor began trying to be as helpful to the General as he could. "Would you like me to play it for you?"

"Yes...I think I would. What did they do yesterday, or I should say last night?" He asked.

"Mostly medical examinations, sir. Major Barkley took a lot of samples and conducted physicals on them."

"That sounds fine. Let me see that tape."

The young sailor took the tape and placed it in a VCR that was not in use. He indicated the monitor that would display the recording.

"Thank you son," the General said. "Perhaps you should return to your station. If I need anything else, I will let you know."

"Yes sir," he said and returned to his seat where he observed the monitors and went back to entering information into his logbook.

The video displayed the scene of what appeared to be any ordinary person getting a physical with the exception that this man was wearing a collar around his neck of some sort. The man on the screen in the blue jumpsuit sat on the table as the doctor examined him, then drew blood for testing. The General felt disappointed at this initial view of what he had risked so much for; he had imagined more of a beast with dominant features or bulging biceps or something. But instead he appeared to be a plain man, the skin color slightly paler than an average human.

How would these creatures help him? Where were the powers that they were supposed to have? How could they help him in achieving his goal? Had he been wrong in pursuing this action without a field test that would have confirmed or denied what they thought about these creatures? If this information ever leaked out, he would be finished and retirement to some obscure life would be bestowed upon him. This had to work; this had to be the way that the United States would regain its seat of power and world dominance. The U.S. needed to stop taking all the crap from these third world shit-holes that were getting their hands on weapons that threatened the country.

"Found what you're looking for General?" Reese asked as he walked into the control room.

"Commander Reese, how are you?" asked the General. "And no, I haven't seen anything yet that says that they are what you say they are."

"Stick around for feeding time, that's always interesting."

"But what does that prove? They drink blood. It's a strange world out there, Commander. I need something more."

"Unfortunately we didn't have a video recording of the initial attack when one of them took out two SEALs as if they were children."

"They could have been careless and him just lucky," the General said with a shrug. "We need some kind of test of their abilities."

"Why the hurry? We've only been here for a few days."

"Do you have any idea how much this is costing, Commander?" the General asked sharply. "I can understand your personal interest because of your background in studying these...creatures or whatever they are. But I need something to keep the money flowing."

Reese had no response to that. He knew the costs must have been staggering for the resources expended on the capture and the captivity—taxpayer dollars at work. And he had to admit that his personal interest was greater than his military interest. For now the key thing was to keep the general engaged with what was happening. Keep him interested.

"I understand sir. If I may suggest, perhaps we should get the doctor's briefing and Lieutenant Johnson's report. Then we can figure out our next move."

"Fine."

"How about some breakfast first?" Reese asked. "The briefing is not scheduled for another two hours and this is probably going to be a long day.

"Lead on, Commander." Reese led the General into the small dining area within the facility. The Navy cook on duty took their orders and the General and Reese sat down at an isolated table. Reese drank a large cup of coffee; he had been up all night with the creatures and was fighting exhaustion with the caffeine. He had assumed he was going to be able to grab a couple of hours of sleep since the General was not scheduled to show up until nine. But here he was.

"So tell me, Commander, are you still thinking about retiring in a year or so?"

"Yes sir." Reese was caught off guard by the personal question.

"Why?"

"Time for a change. I've been thinking about teaching, maybe even writing a book," Reese said as he felt his guard drop at the unusual interest the General was showing in his life.

"A book? What kind?"

"A comparative work of myth and folklore and how they are related to the current day world."

"Sounds interesting. And how appropriate for you that you are involved with this operation."

"You could say that sir," Reese answered.

"I just did, Commander." The General's tone changed. He became irritated, his eyes darting back and forth rapidly. He leaned close to Reese's face. "You realize that you cannot write anything about this operation until it is declassified, if it ever is."

"Yes sir, I understand that," Reese answered. He would not let himself be lured into complacency by the general's personal questions again.

"Good." The General re-seated himself. "Just wanted to be sure of that because if you weren't, I would have to remove you from this operation."

The matter-of-fact tone the General had used made Reese think that the man would do whatever he had to in order to reach the desired end he wanted.

"What are your intentions with these creatures? I read the note you placed in the briefing package you gave me when I was heading to Kosovo and I have to admit, it was somewhat disturbing," said Reese.

"Oh that," the General said in a casual tone again. "I just wanted to get you thinking that's all. Pretty wild thoughts huh?"

"Yes sir."

The cook brought their food to them. They ate in silence, although it was obvious that they were both deep in thought. Reese found it hard to take his gaze from the glass of tomato juice that the General drank greedily.

THE BRIEFING was in the main conference room of the facility. Commander Reese and General Stone entered and found Commander Scott, Lieutenant Johnson, and Major Barkley present. They all rose as the General entered.

"Carry on gentleman," the General barked. "I'm in the mood for some good news and I hate to be disappointed. Who wants to start?"

"I think the medical aspect is the most relevant," said Reese. "Major Barkley, please begin."

"Yes sir," he said hesitantly, his eyes reflected an uncertainty that obviously had him considering his manner of presentation and approach. "My report is not as conclusive as I would like."

Reese figured Barkley would cut to the heart of the matter.

"These creatures have had a full battery of blood work and analysis along with standard motor control and flexibility tests. They have the best dexterity and motor control movement that I have ever seen. If I were to guess I would say that they have the strength and endurance of three to five men, maybe more. All of their senses are highly acute, much more than our own."

"That's extraordinary," said General Stone.

"Yes sir, it is. But," he began with hesitancy in his voice, "I cannot tell you why they have this ability. Or why that if you inflict a minor injury to them that it heals incredibly fast. During the blood work, by the time I filled one tube and went to inject the next, the hole healed up and closed."

"Perfect," the General said, elated.

"So they cannot be killed?" asked Commander Scott.

"They can die," said Barkley. "We put a vile of the blood out in the sunlight, and it boiled itself off in a matter of seconds. Their bodies cannot recover from massive wounds. If they were close enough to an explosion it could kill them by decapitation or severe dismemberment."

"How did you determine that?" Scott asked.

"The one called Dimitri, he said that he saw one of them killed that way during World War II," said Reese.

"World War II?" asked the General.

"Yes sir, from what we have been able to determine from what they have told us so far and by the tests, they are more than a hundred years old."

"Amazing! But doctor, surely there must be some explanation for these attributes?"

"Their blood has to be the key. It is quite different. Unlike ours, it has no living cells. The living cells they ingest from the blood from a living organism, all die, and that causes them to require more living blood to sustain them. That is how the cycle works, or at least how I believe it works. You have to understand General that this is all new ground we are covering."

"Something in them causes the blood to die?" Reese asked.

"That's my guess. They don't use the organs that they were born with or not in any way that I can tell. They don't require food or water to live nor do they require to relieve their bodies of any waste."

"What about reproduction organs?" asked Commander Scott.

"They no longer function. As far as how that works, perhaps Commander Reese would be more of an authority."

"They breed," said Reese, "according to legend and myth, by taking a human to the point of death by draining the blood from them. Then that human drinks the dead blood from the creature and that begins the cycle of transformation. The creature that created them becomes the master and those that were created are subservient. This is purely legend, but hopefully I can learn if this is in fact. I have had conversations with Dimitri that indicates someone called Alexander created them. But he was killed in World War Two.

"So Major Barkley, what you are telling me is that we cannot figure out what gives them the power that they possess?" asked General Stone.

"Not at this time sir," answered Barkley. "And if I may speculate, I don't believe there is a medical reason for it."

The General looked incredulous. "There must be a reason why they are the way they are. You're not going to go off in some mumbo-jumbo area, are you?"

Barkley glanced at Reese then spoke. "Some things go beyond normal reasoning and medicine, sir. I don't believe we'll find a scientific explanation."

"Are you positive there is no way to duplicate or replicate these powers?"

"Not without subscribing to their method of reproduction that Commander Reese spoke about."

"Thank you Major," said the General. He turned to Lieutenant Johnson. "Your report, Johnson."

"During their physicals, we installed a more advanced collar device. It provides a range of two to three miles so if they tried to escape, the devices will activate from a safe distance. It also has a more sensitive anti-removal device. There is available technology that would increase this function if we so choose to use it. The elixir that was developed by the civilian is an obvious deterrent against them trying anything against us. We have positive control over distance as long as we have potent elixir or as long as the creatures believe it to be."

"Have we learned to duplicate it yet?" asked the General.

"Not quite," said Reese. "Idriz has production methods that we have not been able to duplicate yet. He insists on playing an active part of the control of the creatures; a way of taunting them with death because they killed his daughters out of a blood feud between the creatures and his family. I had to promise him that he could speak with the creature known as Josip in order to get him to produce a new batch of elixir. He's also agreed to put together explicit instructions on its development."

"Offer him money," said the General with a wave of his hand.

"It's not money he wants, General," said Reese. "I think he wants to inflict as much pain as possible on the creatures."

"I'll talk to him," the General said. "I'll get him to see reason. Besides if he keeps the fear in the creatures, then all the better for us in using and controlling them."

Reese was about to object, but thought he would save his reservations for another time when he was alone with the General.

"Are there any other comments?" asked the General.

"I have one," said Reese. "Just a note of concern. All security measures must be adhered to—to ensure the creatures aren't allowed to get any human blood."

"Of course not, Commander," said the General said with an exaggerated air of shock. "Aside from the obvious reason, do you have any other concerns in this matter?"

"From what we can tell, these creatures have subsisted mainly on animal blood. It's possible that the taking of human blood causes a development of a superiority complex, and makes them more dangerous."

"Thank you, Commander. Are there any more questions?"

The men fell silent.

"So gentleman, from what I am hearing, we have positive control over these creatures and we should be able to control them and to put them through a operational test."

"An operational test to determine what?" asked Reese.

"Any military benefit," said the General. "Why else have we gone through all of this?"

Reese did not answer. Instead he glanced at Johnson whose face was, as usual, emotionless as he stared straight ahead.

"We'll arrange a test for tonight; something simple but enough to show us what they can do."

LIEUTENANT JOHNSON and Commander Reese sat in the common area with Dimitri and his men.

"They have arranged a test for you and your men," Reese said to

Dimitri. "You are to attack a defensive position that has been set up, penetrate inside, kill the target, and return without being detected."

"A game?" asked Dimitri.

"In a way," said Reese. "Lieutenant Johnson will brief you on the particulars of the mission."

"They want to see how their specimens work, is that it?" Dimitri smiled. A chuckle came from Josip who had so far remained silent.

"If you don't go through with it, there will be no sense in maintaining this facility."

"A threat?" Dimitri eyebrows rose.

"No. Not from me but as I told you earlier, I am not in charge. If there is no benefit derived, then there is no justification for expenditure."

"When do we meet who is in charge?" asked Dimitri.

"Perhaps after the test."

"Then that is reason enough to go through with this charade." Dimitri motioned for his men to assemble around where Lieutenant Johnson waited to show them the specifics of the mission.

"This is the building," Johnson began with military formality as he indicated the position on the map. "You and your men will be dropped off here, approximately two miles away. From there you make your way through their outlying defenses. After that, there are guards stationed at these areas," he indicated red X's that had been marked on the map. "Once through them, there are motion detectors here, here, and here." He pointed to areas he had circled on the map. "The target will be located somewhere within this building. You will spray him with the paint gun indicating a positive kill, then return to the point that you were dropped at. Any questions?"

"We will be armed with weapons?" asked Josip.

"Paint guns. They shoot a ball of paint that upon impact release their material and mark the person as a confirmed kill."

Josip laughed at the explanation and received a stern look from Dimitri.

"Clothing and equipment will be provided to each of you. We leave within the hour for the drop-off point."

"I know how fast you are," warned Reese. "But you cannot hide from the tracking devices in your collars. Any deviation from the direction of the target will result in activation of the devices."

Dimitri looked at Reese curiously. "And whose finger will be poised on the button?"

"Get ready to go."

TWO HOURS later, Dimitri and his men were dropped at the specified spot near the oceanfront of the base.

"I'll wait here. Good luck," said Johnson, but received no responses.

The four men headed off until they were out of direct sight of Lieutenant Johnson, then stopped.

"We play this madness?" Josip asked incredulous as he held out the weapon in front of him.

"For now," answered Dimitri. "Remember, learn what we can from them and when we are ready, we will disappear. Let's give them a good show."

Josip did not respond, but Dimitri could feel his gaze upon him as he indicated the direction for them to go. They moved swiftly and without sound. They passed through the first line of defenses easily. There were six men armed with night-vision goggles, but Dimitri and his men gave off no heat that would allow them to be detected. They approached the building that held their target. The four men crouched together outside the beams of strong light that penetrated the darkness and illuminated the approach to the building.

"You will take the guards out with the paint guns," Dimitri indicated to Andre and Iliga. "Scale the walls where they are not looking, they do not expect an attack from their walled areas because it offers no grips for anyone to climb. We will wait here until you give the sign that all is clear, then you act like guards while Josip and I go inside. And remember," Dimitri said putting an arm on each of their shoulders, "do not injure them, understand?"

They nodded and moved off. Dimitri and Josip waited in the darkness. Dimitri was confident that they would do as they were told. He had Josip to stay with him so he could keep an eye on his ill-tempered friend.

"We could have marched in the front entrance and killed them before they knew what was happening. Why do we waste time?"

"Yes we could have," Dimitri agreed. "But we don't want to give away all our secrets now, do we? All we have to do is enough to get the job done."

Josip smiled at Dimitri's cunning as the signal from Andre and Iliga was given.

"Let's go," said Dimitri.

They passed by the motion detectors and entered the building. There was a guard seated at a desk. A radio blared as he wrote in a logbook. Dimitri indicated for Josip to take him. Josip moved forward just as the guard looked up, Josip locked his eyes onto his and the guard did not move as Josip moved forward. When he was close, he raised and fired the paint gun at the mesmerized guard.

As the red paint dripped from the guard's clothing, Josip said, "You're dead," and he bared his exposed fangs to the man. "Be quiet now and just lay there or I will get angry." Josip said as his eyes focused on the dark red paint with longing and licked his lips with his tongue. The guard watched in fear as Josip inched closer.

"Enough," Dimitri said. "Let's finish this." He pointed toward the interior of the building. They moved forward, their feet not making any sound.

Within minutes they heard voices coming from a room, two doors down in the corridor. They passed by the first and went into the second. The men in the room gazed up startled by their appearance and went for their weapons. But Dimitri moved quickly in their path surprising them and painted them with bursts from the pain gun.

"Which of you is the designated target?" asked Dimitri.

"We're dead," one of them said as they lay on the ground. But Dimitri noticed the smiles on their faces instead of looks of defeat.

"Josip!" Dimitri yelled, realizing that they had made a mistake. "Check the room we passed."

Instead of going back the way he came, Josip charged the wall that joined the two rooms. He smashed through the wood and dry wall to find two more men preparing to exit through a door that led to the outside. He grabbed them both, one by each hand, and threw them toward the way that he had come through the broken wall. They landed a few feet from where Dimitri stood. Josip charged toward them, his face enraged with fury that Dimitri knew meant trouble.

"Stop!" Dimitri cried, but Josip kept coming with a red rage that filled his eyes. His teeth were bared and his fingernails had elongated into sharp claws. As he moved toward the nearest man, Dimitri slapped Josip with a force that sent him flying. Josip got up, and Dimitri saw that the rage had passed, at least for the moment.

Dimitri motioned for Josip to go out in the corridor and wait. When he was gone, Dimitri used the paint gun on the two men to confirm the kills that would end this part of the charade and then threw the weapon on the ground in disgust.

"Let's go," He told Josip as he entered into the corridor. "I trust there will be no more outbursts?"

Josip shook his head and said, "I guess I got a little excited."

"Yes, I believe you did. But if you don't learn to control your temper, we will all be killed. They must believe they have us under control. I don't want them to know the full range of our strengths or weaknesses."

"I understand," Josip said, obviously incensed by his own behavior. "I will do better."

"Let's get Andre and Iliga and get back. We have done what we had to do. The show is over for the moment."

On their trip back to their pick-up point, Dimitri indicated for Andre and Iliga to take out the guards. He knew that this was not necessary, but would give an appearance that they were bragging or that they were vain about their abilities. A weakness the Americans would think they might be able to use against them.

They met Lieutenant Johnson and their transport vehicle at the pick-up point. Johnson was surprised to see them so soon. He looked at his watch and then at them. He had not expected them for at least an hour.

"How the hell did you do that so..." He stopped his statement when he realized the senselessness of it.

"Please take us back," Dimitri began ignoring the half-finished statement. "My men are hungry after expending so much energy. It is time for us to feed. The feast of the victors, wouldn't you say, Lieutenant Johnson?" Dimitri wanted to learn more about this military man. Find out what his weaknesses were that they could use against him later. The Lieutenant's reaction to their return indicated both surprise and awe. This would be the beginning of determining how they could use him.

Johnson looked at the group with admiration that he usually held in reserve. They had completed their task, successful and in a mere fraction of the amount of time that he anticipated. No red splotches of paint stained their clothing.

"From one warrior to another," Dimitri began. "We both have an appreciation for the art of military tactics."

"Yes," Johnson said. He closed the back of the vehicle and took his place in the cab with the driver. He instructed the driver to return to the facility. As the vehicle made its way back, Johnson realized that he had never felt such admiration for a group of men.

CHAPTER 13

"I'D CALL THAT a damned successful test," General Stone said. "In fact, with a little training in tactics they could be operational in no time." He looked at Commander Reese, Commander Stone, Lieutenant Johnson, and Major Barkley as they sat in the briefing room going over the results of the test.

"Lieutenant Johnson," he said. "From an operational platoon commander, what is your assessment?"

Johnson hesitated before he spoke, glancing sideways to find Reese's stern gaze pinning him.

"They achieved the objective above expected parameters that were set for them. Our own forces could not have performed as well."

"Commander Reese, any comment?"

Reese thought about what Dimitri had said when he told them about the test. To see how their specimens acted.

"General, I concur with the findings and results of the test, however I think that if any further thoughts as to the use of this team in the future is to have any success, then some type of terms will have to be arranged with them."

"What are you talking about?"

"I don't think that the threat of death for not performing what you dictate to them will have the effect you desire. I would suggest a—"

"I have a way of finding the weak points in people, Commander," the General said interrupting Reese. "Once I talk to them, I'll figure out something."

"Then may I suggest that now might be a good time? That was the bargain I struck with them in order to go on this test mission," Reese interjected boldly.

The General eyed Reese speculatively. "We shouldn't keep them waiting." The General turned toward the rest of the men and said, "Thank you gentlemen for your time. Commander Reese, take me to our friends."

They proceeded toward the confinement area of the creatures. Reese wondered what the General would use for leverage against them.

The look the General had in his eyes as he saw the creatures complete the mission was one of awe and enthusiasm. He had plans in his mind; there was no doubt about that. And Johnson was acting different. Reese wasn't sure what it was, but something made him feel that way.

As they turned the final corner, Idriz Laupki was waiting outside the door along with his interpreter, Corporal Brosnev. Reese felt his stomach lurch at the sight of him knowing that he wanted access now, as was the agreement of their bargain.

Earlier, Major Barkley informed Reese that he had received a new batch of the elixir with explicit instructions on how to make it. Idriz had lived up to his half of the bargain, now Reese would have to live up to his.

Reese made introductions and the interpreter translated, but Idriz made no response, instead he pointed at his throat.

"He has laryngitis," the Corporal began. "He inhaled some fumes from the new batch of elixir that he made. It caused his throat to become sore and he lost his voice. Major Barkley said it would be temporary."

"Please pass along my personal thanks for the good work he has been doing for us," the General said to the Corporal who quickly translated it. Idriz smiled but emitted no sound. "He is welcome to join us, I know that was part of the bargain for the work he has done."

Again the translator spoke and Idriz bowed his head to the General's request.

"Sir, perhaps now is not the best time," said Reese.

"Are you telling me it is not safe, Commander? All these safeguards you have should be more then enough."

"No sir, that's not the problem," said Reese. He lowered his voice so that only the General would hear him. "It's just that there is bad blood between this man and the creatures, if you intend to bargain..."

"Bargain? No commander, I don't intend to bargain," he said, his cheeks flushed with anger. "I think you used the correct word earlier. I plan to dictate to them. Now let's go."

Reese hesitated before sliding his card and pressing his thumbprint to the scanner and turned toward the Corporal.

"Corporal, you stay out here. Call Lieutenant Johnson for me and tell him to meet us here."

"Yes sir."

The door slid open and the three men entered. The Corporal was on the phone locating Lieutenant Johnson, as one of the guards stood watch at the door. As they entered the common area, they found the creatures sitting and talking amongst themselves.

Dimitri rose to meet them and placed a hand on Josip's shoulder so that he would stay seated. Reese saw a look pass between the two creatures. Dimitri was nervous about something, probably about the presence of the Idriz Laupki, just as Reese was.

"Dimitri," said Reese, "this is General Stone. He is in charge of what happens around here."

"Ah...general it is an honor to meet you. But if I may suggest, this other man," he said pointing at Idriz, "should not be in here. It is not a good time."

"This man is part of my team," the General said setting the tone for the conversation. "And if I want him—"

"Forgive me General, but my men have been on your little test and they are wound up. It happens sometimes and it takes a while for them to calm down. The sight of this man—"

"Who do you think you are?" boomed the General. "You can't tell me who I can bring in here."

"It is him," Josip said. "The one that killed Franjo. He comes in here to taunt us with that fact."

Idriz smiled but did not say anything as he locked gazes with Josip. Then he said something in his native tongue that Reese did not understand, but it was clear that Josip understood perfectly.

What the hell? Surprise flooded Reese. Idriz was supposed to have lost his voice, and yet he sounded clear as always. Josip rose from his chair and was at Idriz before Reese had blinked. His hands clasped the man's throat, but Idriz still smiled even as Josip slit it open with his long fingernail. Blood flowed a deep red down Idriz's throat as Josip began to drink voraciously. Idriz laughed and Reese saw his tongue coated with blood.

Reese awoke from the stupor and turned to the observation window of the control room.

"Activate the—"

Before Reese finished his sentence, Josip screamed, dropping Idriz onto the ground. Lieutenant Johnson and his standby security team burst into the room and surrounded the remaining three creatures. Idriz fell into a heap, blood still squirting from the main artery in his throat. Josip's skin began to burn. Tiny flames consumed his flesh.

Major Barkley came in after Johnson and his men. He knelt over Idriz, searching for a pulse in the mess of flesh that had been his neck.

"He's dead," Barkley said.

Reese turned to Josip who was now a lump of burning flesh.

None of the other creatures moved to help him because it would do no good. Josip was doomed as soon as the elixir had entered into his body. Dimitri knelt at the side of his friend, shaking his head as the blood-filled tears flowed down his cheeks. Andre and Iliga joined him, placing their hands on his shoulder and not saying a word.

General Stone appeared unaffected at the event that had taken only seconds to transpire. But Reese thought that beneath that stoic demeanor, he was plotting and planning even as death lay within five feet of him. He had now seen up close the capability of his new team that now found itself short one member.

Reese turned to Johnson. "My compliments to the control room. They activated the collar just—"

"They didn't. I told them to hold off until I was in the room and signaled. I was going to try and resolve the conflict before ordering the activation."

"But if the collar wasn't activated, how did the elixir get released?"

Major Barkley looked up from Idriz's body. "I think Idriz drank the elixir. His throat and mouth tissues show signs of massive bleeding. There is scar tissue, too. He's been drinking the elixir for a while."

"He goaded Josip into attacking," said Dimitri. "Just as he did to Franjo with the poisoned cow...except this time, he was the bait."

"What are you talking about?" asked the general.

"Idriz knew that if he could get into this room, he would have a chance to kill Josip," answered Reese. "He saturated his body with the elixir, then said something to Josip to rile him. He knew that if Josip attacked, either the control room would activate the collar, or Josip would get the elixir from him. Either way, he got what he wanted. Revenge."

"PLEASE ACCEPT my apology for the loss of your friend," the General said to Dimitri as the two of them sat in a conference room. General Stone had thought it best to talk to Dimitri alone against protests from Reese and Johnson. "We did not expect the man to act the way he did. But he has paid the price."

"Is that supposed to be some kind of conciliation?"

"No, of course not. But I saw in the reports from Commander Reese that Josip attacked and killed two other men. I would surmise that it was only a matter of time before he would have tried to kill others."

Dimitri looked into the cold hard eyes of the General. He knew that he was here to not offer his sympathy, but to get to the heart of what he wanted.

"Possibly," Dimitri answered. "But no one should have to die like that." He added, "Especially a soldier," to see the General's reaction,

The General stared at Dimitri with a curious look and said, "A soldier?"

"Yes, that is what we were, more in spirit than in body, but soldiers of our country nonetheless."

"You wanted to fight to keep your country from the invading bastards, isn't that correct?" asked the General.

"Yes," said Dimitri and saw the look in the General's eyes that he wanted. He had led him in the direction he wanted.

"Things are not the same anymore as they were in the time you marched off to fight. Politics have worsened. The soldiers become the politician's puppets."

"Ah," Dimitri said. "There is the obvious battleground and there is the other."

"Yes. You understand."

"What is it you want from me and my men?"

"I want you to fight for my country," he blurted out as if the words had been waiting too long for him to use.

"Fight? But how can we turn the great tide of the west for you? You have the strongest force in the world today."

"That is true, but we cannot use them where we need to because of political borders that have been set up to protect the rich and bureaucratic assholes of the world."

"And where are these borders?" asked Dimitri.

"Many places, but first I would attack those that are nearest to us. Those that send their drugs into our country. Drugs that people use to kill themselves."

"It sounds like a noble cause that you carry upon your shoulder, but..."

"But what?"

"Surely this cannot be sanctified by your politicians."

"No, of course not. This would be a clandestine operation. I would be in charge of the team. I would pick the missions, outfit you and your men with whatever you need."

"And why should we go along with you?"

"You said you are a soldier."

"Yes."

"You cannot help your own country. They need to settle their internal squabbles. But you can help mine. You can rid the world of those that prey on humanity. And when that is done and things have settled down in your own country, I'll send you back, well-trained and prepared for modern warfare."

"A truly noble cause."

"And you can have all the human blood of the enemy you want," the General added. "I will afford you every accommodation that you may desire, within reason of course."

"An attractive proposition."

"It is, considering the other option," the General added coldly.

"Death."

The General said nothing, then nodded. Dimitri appeared to think it over even though his mind had been made up before they had began the conversation.

"It appears that your offer to utilize our talents for the good of your country is the best option of the two."

"I thought you would agree."

"There is something else we would like. We have been out of touch for a very long time. We have an idea of what the world is like around us, but much is sketchy. We would like to be taught how things have progressed; especially the technological advancements."

"So you want to go back to school, so to speak."

"Yes, and we would like Commander Reese to be our teacher."

"Why Reese?"

"He best understands our background and can build upon that."

"I'll think about it. Commander Reese is not exactly on the same line of thought as I am on certain matters."

"And the man called Johnson. Will he remain our operational point of contact? I ask that because he, too, is familiar with us and understands us."

"Johnson is a good man. He stays and will be team leader on all operations."

"Excellent," Dimitri said. "We will treat him as one of our own."

"Then we have come to terms?"

"Yes," Dimitri said and held out his hand.

The General smiled as he accepted his hand, but the smile quickly faded as he felt the coldness of Dimitri's hand touch his.

"It is time to feed. Would you care to join us?" Dimitri smiled, his fangs barely showing.

"No, thank you."

Dimitri waited for someone to escort him back. While he waited he thought to himself how times had changed and now how they must as well. *We use each other to attain our goals, but your thinking General is long term...and mine is much shorter.*

"IT'S ALL arranged," General Stone said to Commander Reese and Lieutenant Johnson. "Dimitri and I have come to an agreement."

"An agreement?" asked Reese.

"Yes. He has agreed to use his men in support of...covert surveillance."

"Surveillance?" Reese questioned. "After what happened a few hours ago, you think you can trust them?"

"Yes I do. He will use his men in the ways that I specify to benefit the United States, and in return they will survive. He is a patriot in a way, from a different time and place but a patriot all the same."

"General," said Reese. "Do you actually think—"

"Commander if you wish to remain on this special assignment, you had better adjust your attitude and go along with the program."

Reese fell silent, his cheeks flushing in anger.

"Your services have been requested as an instructor. Your job will be to bring them up to speed with the world as it is. Can you handle that, Commander, or do I need to find someone else?"

"I can handle it," Reese replied flatly.

"Good. You are dismissed. I want to speak to Lieutenant Johnson."

"Yes sir," Reese replied and gave a sideward glance at Johnson, who continued to look ahead, his eyes fixed on the General. Reese exited the room and closed the door.

"Have a seat, Lieutenant," the General said indicating the chair next to him, then he sat. "What is your opinion of this whole operation? Be honest."

"We have an uncertain potential for the use of these creatures," said Johnson. "I say uncertain because unless they truly cooperate, any benefit derived will be useless."

"A good point," said the General. "And what do you think about Commander Reese?"

"He's not an operator, sir. He has background knowledge from his association with the teams, but nothing practical to actual operations. However, these creatures are here, and without Reese's help, we would not have captured them. He lacks the Special Forces intuition, but could be trained. Until that time, he would be out of his league."

"I would agree, but the creatures relate to him. I will keep him on until he becomes a hindrance, but he will not be involved with the operational side unless I decide he needs to be. Is that understood?"

"Yes, sir."

"How about you?"

"Sir?"

"I have a few questions for you before I decide if you stay on this project or not," he said. "What do you think of them, the creatures?"

"I am fascinated by them. The more I am around them and see them operate I find myself becoming more in tuned to them in a way. Almost envious."

"Envious? How so?"

"They are almost indestructible. Their lightning-fast reflexes and highly tuned senses make them a formidable adversary."

"And their blood thirst? Do you find that envious also?"

"It seems a reasonable price to pay for their attributes and for the price of mortality," Johnson said without reservation, which surprised the General.

"Very well. Now how about them killing human beings. How do you feel about that?"

"Depends of whom we were talking about sir."

"The enemy, of course."

"Then that would be a casualty of war, a fact of life for a warrior or soldier," Johnson said coldly.

"My feelings exactly. I want you to be team leader. Go on the missions and use them as I specify. Can you live with that?"

"Yes sir."

"Can you direct them to kill?"

"Yes sir."

"To kill and feed off of their prey?"

"Yes sir."

"Very good, Lieutenant. Now I have one final question for you. You understand the need to keep something like this confidential?"

"Yes sir."

"If the information got into the wrong hands, there could be trouble."

"Yes sir."

"You would do whatever was needed to prevent that, wouldn't you?"

"Of course, sir."

"Good. I think we have an arrangement." The General shook

Johnson's hand, glad to feel the warmth unlike Dimitri's handshake. "I want you to begin their training in tactics. They almost got caught from behind in the test mission. Their strength and cunning saved them but I don't want to take any chances."

"Is there a particular strategy that you want me to follow?"

"Stay in the infiltration and assassination mode of operation," he said. "But if Commander Reese or anyone else asks, fall back to the surveillance cover. If you need anything, contact Commander Scott and he will get it for you. Understand?"

"Yes sir."

"That's all. I'll be in touch."

Johnson turned and left the room, as he closed the door behind him, he couldn't remember feeling so exhilarated before in his life.

REESE ENTERED into the secure area where he found Dimitri sitting in a corner, appearing to be deep in thought. Andre and Iliga were sitting at a table playing a game of chess, their gazes riveted to the pieces on the board.

"Sold your soul again, didn't you?" Reese asked. "Does it get easier over time?"

"Everything gets easier over time," answered Dimitri. "Especially if you have all the time that there is. And I do. Most humans live such a short span of time that they do not learn that life is a battle of compromise. Those that think they can control everything, fall to the death of illusion. Those that bend with the changes do not break, they adapt and learn how to survive for an uncomfortable period of time knowing that it will be worth the wait."

"Philosophy? You quote philosophy at a time like this?"

"And what were we suppose to do Commander?" Dimitri asked. "You know what the other option was, and death does not appeal to me. We have already lost one of us since we have been here." Silence settled between them. Reese found it hard to not feel somewhat responsible; if they had been left in their own environment, Josip and Idriz might still be alive.

"You're having an attack of conscience?" Dimitri asked. "You orchestrated our capture."

"I didn't think there was any truth to the story of your discovery when I got the assignment. I thought it would turn out to be just another explained mystery or that the General was just being eccentric. When it turned out to be true, people depended on me to get the mission done. All I wanted was to study you and learn about what life for you is like."

"So you sought your own personal gain from us, just as the General seeks his own. Does that make you any different from him?"

"He has other plans. I know that and so do you. I would venture to say that his are a bit more involved than what I had in mind. Would you care to describe this arrangement he has with you and what it entails?"

"You will be our teacher, to bring us into the current time. And in exchange, I will teach you about what I know. A fair exchange wouldn't you say?"

"So you won't tell me then? The specifics that you and the General have worked out?"

"No. It would only get you removed from this position," Dimitri said in a matter-of-fact tone. "The General and I have an understanding between us in a way that I feel comfortable with. Besides, this arrangement will be good for both of us, we learn more about this new world, you learn more about our kind, and the General gets what he wants. Perfect symmetry. You aren't going to upset the balance and miss the opportunity of a lifetime, are you?"

Reese exhaled in frustration as he stuffed his hands into his pockets and walked around the room shuffling his feet. Dimitri watched him with a look of amusement.

"Okay," Reese finally said. "I give up. You said compromise was a good thing to learn."

"It is for those that must."

Reese smiled, then said, "What do you want to learn about?"

"All about the world. Start first with the United States and this area; we might as well learn about our new home."

REESE RETURNED to his quarters as morning approached. He was becoming more acquainted with the night/day routine and longed for his apartment and his bed, but after his discussion with Dimitri on this latest turn of events, he knew that sleep would not come easily.

He wasn't sure if it was an attack of conscience as Dimitri had said, or that he felt that he couldn't trust the General to misuse these creatures in some macabre manner. And the images of the deaths of Idriz and Josip refused to leave his thoughts. The operation was becoming like a bad dream that kept escalating as each night went by, and getting closer to some dreaded event that lie at the end.

He heard the door to the room next to him open and close. Lieutenant Johnson must have returned. He left his own room and knocked on the door. Johnson answered.

"Got a minute?" Reese asked.

"Sure, come on in." Reese entered as Johnson offered him a chair. They both sat.

"So," Reese began. "I understand that you are in charge of the team."

"Purely from an operational standpoint, Commander. You can see the purpose in that, can't you?"

"Of course," Reese said detecting something peculiar in the voice of Johnson. "So what's next then?"

"Training. I am going to teach them tactics in warfare and bring them up to speed on detection equipment and the like. They are going to be a surveillance team for deep cover missions."

"Surveillance?"

"Yes," Johnson said, offering no further explanation.

Reese studied the face of the man in front of him and saw how it had changed in the past couple of days. He appeared haggard and his face had a withdrawn look, but his eyes seemed more alive than Reese remembered since the operation had started. His words sounded rehearsed as if he was using scripted answers.

"You've changed," Reese began. "You're not letting this all get to you are you? The creatures and the General?"

"No, of course not. I am fascinated by the creatures," he said, as his eyes seemed to glimmer.

"They are fascinating."

"Ever since I watched them perform the test mission—the way they move and blend in to their surroundings—it's as if they were made for it."

"Survival instincts," Reese said. "All creatures have them to an extent in order that they can survive."

"Survival of the fittest. The weak shall perish and only the strong remain to carry on."

"Yes, something like that."

"Why do suppose they never took over the world?" asked Johnson.

"Tough question. You have to remember that until a few days ago, we weren't even sure that they existed at all."

"Speculate," he asked, his tone close to demanding an answer.

"It's mainly from a standpoint of control. If the master has many under him, he could be challenged for control and the chances of losing it would be greater. There is no reference to any large groups that indicates that they prefer it that way. I have read that they basically stake their ground so to speak and will chase out any other vampire that might enter it, as a manner of protecting their food supply."

"Territorial."

"Exactly," Reese agreed and rose to leave. "It's late and we both need some rest. I must be going."

"Wait a minute, please," Johnson asked as he reached for Reese's arm. "Just one more question."

"All right," Reese said surprised at Johnson's interest. He sat back down.

"What if they weren't that way, say someone had brought them all together to form a large group and descended on humanity town by town, making more creatures. And the cycle kept on going and going. Wouldn't the world be an interesting place today?"

"Interesting?" Reese asked. "No I wouldn't say that. I wouldn't even want to imagine something like that. Why?"

"Just thinking."

"If you want some advice, you need to back away from thoughts like that. These creatures and their talents are consuming you. This whole affair is crazy and you better watch out for General Stone. He has plans within plans and I don't trust him. He strikes me as the kind of person that would do whatever it takes to get something done, regardless of the cost."

"Of course he would," Johnson said. "He's a soldier. His main concern is with the protection of this country against all enemies foreign and domestic. That is what the military is supposed to do. You do remember that oath, Commander, don't you?"

"Of course I do," Reese snapped. "But as with most things, these commitments come with morals and conscience. We do not act blindly without considering the consequence of our actions."

"Enough!"

"What the hell has gotten into you? It's the General isn't it? He's gotten to you, hasn't he?" Reese asked. "Filled your mind with enough patriotic flavor to hide the real taste of what he has in mind. What does he really have planned?"

"Good night, Commander," Johnson said as he opened the door. "It's late and, as you said, we are both tired. Our passions seem to be getting the best of us."

"Look Johnson, Dimitri and the others gave up their souls more than a hundred years ago so that they could continue to live. They didn't have any choice in the matter. You do," Reese said pointing at him as he exited the room. The door was slammed shut. Reese went into his room, closed his door, and lay on the bunk but did not sleep for a long time.

CHAPTER 14

THE SCHEDULE for the next couple of weeks became a set routine whereby Dimitri and his men spent their first four hours after waking with Lieutenant Johnson, learning tactics and the art of warfare in the twenty-first century. The next couple of hours were feeding and free time, then they ended the night with Commander Reese and their education. They usually ended up in a philosophical debate before they were finished.

During this time, the relationship between Reese and Johnson was cold and neither spoke to the other. But Johnson appeared to be enthusiastic and energetic in his work with the creatures as they held classes, conducted exercises in the field, and used mock demos of facilities to put into use what they were learning. The creatures were excellent students and learned exceptionally fast. Johnson could not have been more pleased and in further awe at their abilities.

"Your time is better than yesterday," Johnson said to Dimitri as he checked his stopwatch. They emerged from the mock set-up they had arranged within the facility.

"Once we learn the proper motion, we constantly improve upon it. It is our way," Dimitri said.

"You never tire, do you?"

"Of course we do, but it is only from a lack of sustenance, not from physical exertion."

"Fascinating." Johnson stared at Dimitri and noticed he was not breathing heavy. "If we had more like you, we could end a lot of the problems in the world today."

"I think you would have more problems rather than less," Dimitri countered. "We have been learning about history and this new world in which we live. It becomes apparent that those who do not have something that the other side does, will take extraordinary measures to attain it. If they cannot duplicate it, the solution is to get something that is better than the other side has. This escalation is what gets out of hand and leads to more and more trouble."

"But that's what it is all about. It's always a question of who is stronger and that prevents any attempts if one side knows the other will counter with a superior force. It has always been that way and will always be."

"And where will it all end?"

"One power maintains its dominance through this superiority and by that dominance, keeps the peace."

"Peace through threat of retaliation—not exactly what I would call a mutual agreed upon peace."

"It works," countered Johnson.

"That would be debatable. To live under constant fear, is like not living," said Dimitri. "And is that much different than having a global dictatorship?"

Johnson mused this over before he answered.

"I am a soldier, not a politician. I carry out the orders I am given and leave policies and procedures to the ambassadors and diplomats."

"But even a soldier has a conscience, does he not?"

"If sacrifices must be made along the way to meet the overall objective, then that is acceptable."

"And you believe this?"

"Of course I do," Johnson answered.

"Then you are more dangerous than I and my men are," Dimitri said. "We may be creatures of unfathomable life, but we possess individual thinking and reasoning that governs our own choices. We accept the consequences of our actions, do you?"

"I do," Johnson said. "I carry out my orders knowing that I am doing the right thing. I have no attack of conscience. I have pledged my life to protecting this country."

"A true patriot. That is very noble. So you are unlike Commander Reese then in that respect."

"How so?"

"He has reservations of what you are doing and what we shall be doing. He, you could say, is having a bad attack of conscience."

"That's his problem, not ours. We know exactly what we are doing, don't we?"

"Of course," Dimitri answered, eyeing Johnson warily.

"You will get all the human blood you want and we get the removal of certain elements that do not agree with the position of this country."

Dimitri nodded although his only thoughts were about how they would be free once again to roam as they chose.

"I believe that is all for this evening then, Lieutenant?"

"Yes," said Johnson. "I'll have them open the door to the yard. I assume you will want to feed before you meet with Commander Reese."

"That is correct. We cannot go to school on an empty stomach." Dimitri smiled. Johnson looked at him with a questioning gaze; Dimitri drew him in farther and farther.

"You are envious of us, aren't you?" Dimitri asked. "Our powers, they attract you?" he asked as his voice sent soothing tones into Johnson's mind.

"Yes...yes they do," Johnson said, in an almost dreamlike trance now.

"The cost does not frighten you?"

"No. It seems a small price to pay for what one would gain," he said as he shook the fuzziness from his mind.

"Perhaps we may talk of this again later. I do not wish to be late for Commander Reese." Dimitri turned away, signaling for Andre and Iliga to follow.

Johnson watched as they departed, never feeling as alone as he did at this very moment.

REESE LOOKED up as his three students entered into the lounge of their living quarters.

"Running a little late tonight," he said as he glanced at his watch and stifled a yawn. As usual, Andre and Iliga said nothing and sat down as Dimitri turned toward Reese.

"Lieutenant Johnson and I were discussing some particulars in regards to our training."

"Such as?" Reese asked, knowing Dimitri would not tell him.

"Little matters of the heart you might say," Dimitri answered and smiled. "What is our subject for this evening, Commander Reese?"

"Your choice," he said. "We've covered all the basics on history, updated your geography and cultural affairs, and brought you up to date on political affairs."

"How about some philosophy?"

"Specifically what?"

"The freedom of choice."

"Broad area."

"Comparison then," said Dimitri. "There are many groups in your society that are segmented, but are offered special protection from your government and its many agencies almost to an unfair advantage over those that do not have the infliction or special condition."

"Example?"

"Cultural and societal differences. There are laws to protect the religious beliefs of people, the handicapped, minorities, women, terminally ill, AIDS patients. The list goes on and on."

"And?" Reese didn't know where Dimitri was going with this conversation.

"I believe that I could argue a point for myself and my men."

"Really," Reese said incredulous.

"Think about it Commander," Reese began, "Are we not a victim of our circumstance? Or are we just guilty of a maligned thought that at the outset may have looked attractive, and its failings not so important at the time of our creation; and then too late to change our mind and retrace our steps over the threshold that we crossed?"

"None of the categories you mentioned kills in order to survive."

"We do not have to kill in order to survive."

"You yourself said that at times you fed on the less desirable people that wandered your way, the vagabonds, dregs of society that were cast out."

"That is true. But how different is that from man and his ways?"

"What do you mean? Man does not kill like you have."

"No, perhaps not. But what of the wars, the carnage of the third world countries and the righteous acts of the major powers? Has not man killed man under the guise of world peace?"

"Unrelated," Reese countered. "Different circumstances."

"Not really. What of your inner cities then? Some of them are considered murder capitals."

"There are problems. Our culture has spawned our own creatures," Reese conceded. "But how does all this apply to you and your men?"

"We are no different than all these others. We are a product of *our* own culture just as well as those of your cities and man himself. We are no different than anyone else in these categories except that we receive no help, no protection from the government."

"You're stretching it," Reese said although he sounded slightly less convinced then he did earlier.

"All I am saying," said Dimitri, "is that we deserve what the world has to offer and not to be used as pawns in a game that man plays against man."

"This is ludicrous. But I'll humor you. If you were free to go and do whatever you wanted, what would you do?"

"What we have been doing all these years, survive. But survive in our own way, quietly and away from those that would pervert us for their own personal gain." Dimitri paused, and then said, "We may be creatures now, but part of us were men once and still are; we have a need to feel...useful."

Reese looked into the eyes of Dimitri and for the first time he thought he saw human eyes and not those of a creature. He also noticed that Andre and Iliga were looking at him now with what appeared to be keen interest. Normally they showed little curiosity.

"An interesting point," Reese said breaking the silence. "You made several points that would prompt further discussions and considerations. I would even—"

Reese stopped as he heard someone enter the room. He turned and saw Lieutenant Johnson. By the anxious look upon his face, Reese could tell he had some news.

"Commander," he said coolly to Reese, "I hate to interrupt but I need to speak briefly with Dimitri."

"No problem," Reese said, "we're done for the night and it will be dawn soon so I will let you two discuss what you need. Good night," said Reese. He noted that Johnson carried an operational order folder in his hands. *So it begins.*

Johnson waited until Reese left. "We have a assignment," he said as a smile spread across his face. "We leave tomorrow at dusk."

THE MILITARY aircraft landed on the private runway at SOCOM headquarters in Florida in the early hour of the morning. Vehicles met the plane, offloaded the shipping containers, and passengers were escorted to a secure building on the perimeter of the airfield. Within this building, General Stone waited in a conference room.

Lieutenant Johnson and Dimitri entered the room where he waited. Navy SEALs took their usual position, one inside of the room and one outside to maintain their watch on Dimitri in the event they needed to activate the collar.

"Welcome to SOCOM, gentleman," The General greeted them. "Please have a seat and we can get started." Johnson and Dimitri sat as the General opened a folder.

"Our intelligence has located the leaders of several major cocaine distribution networks that route the drugs through Haiti on their way to the States. They, along with other top level associates, are holed up on the island for a limited period of time."

"Local authorities?"

"Not worth a damn. There is almost one hundred percent

corruption in all the enforcement agencies there. As soon as the bulk of our forces pulled out, the gates opened and all the scum of the Earth flowed in. All that we have is our intelligence networks left. The situation is pathetic on the island, but we can't officially do anything without being accused of internal meddling."

"So that is where we come in?" asked Dimitri.

"Yes. You," he said indicating Johnson, "will take in the team and eliminate the entire group," he said without any emotion in his voice. "We figure that at least three are the top officials that hold several organizations together." He handed over three black-and-white photographs. "Eliminate them, and the organizations will crumble into internal fighting and probably be taken over by another group. This will become a game of dominoes as we go along, one leads to another until we get to the last one."

"What's the area like where they are?" Johnson asked. The General drew out an aerial reconnaissance photograph and laid it on the table in front of them.

"It's outside the city of Monte Christi, along the coast. It's an old fortress that was converted into a large private residence that actually serves as a distribution center for the drugs. Take out the leaders, blow the place to hell, and get out. It will be well guarded, but with the stealth that the team has, you should be able to get in undetected.

"Access from the sea will be the way in and out. We have a converted fishing boat standing by for our use. Take a day and familiarize yourselves with the layout and develop your plan as you travel there. You will be flown through the Bahamas and Puerto Rico, only stopping for fuel and then air-dropped the following night to the ship that will be off the coast ready to go in. The ship will bring you back to Puerto Rico where the plane will be waiting. All the details are in your package."

"Equipment?" Johnson asked.

"Everything you need can be obtained from our private stock here; all unmarked, unserialized and untraceable. I've already put the equipment together and it is being loaded on your plane as we speak. Take a look at the list and see if there is anything else you need."

"Yes sir."

"We will need to feed soon," Dimitri added. "Have provisions been made for that?"

"You will feed on the targets," the General said, his grin vicious. "It will add to the hunt, will it not Dimitri?"

Dimitri did not answer as he saw the General was in a mood that was far from reasonable.

"This could be messy and hard to explain," inserted Johnson.

"The messier the better." The General slammed his fist onto the table. "We want to put the fear of God into them. Make them tuck their tails and run home with stories that will make them think twice about coming back. And there will be no explaining because no one is going to claim that the blood was sucked out of the three assholes," he paused looking at Johnson and Dimitri. "Is there a problem with this?" he asked as his gaze focused on Dimitri. "Because if there is, we can activate those collars and end this now."

Dimitri locked his eyes onto the General's with no indication of any emotion in his face. "There is not a problem. It will be done."

"Good then. I'll see you when you get back. Good hunting."

THE FOUR figures came ashore and made their way off the beach. Their target was less than a mile away. At a quick pace, they would arrive in less than fifteen minutes. The plan had been well rehearsed and the need to speak would be avoided at all costs. As they set off, traveling off the road and hiding in the sparse shrubbery, they would not be seen until they were at the small fortress. Each person was dressed the same in their black clothing and carried identical equipment in their black backpacks and watertight bags. Lieutenant Johnson signaled the direction they were to head in and they moved off.

When they arrived at their observing destination, Johnson donned his night vision equipment and surveyed the area. The air reconnaissance photos did not reveal if there were any electronic sensors in place as early alert devices. Johnson scanned the area for telltale signs of the devices but found none and gave the all-clear sign to his team. As he did, he saw from their subtle movements that they were anxious to move in. They were at a heightened state because they had not fed in three days, a fact that Johnson had not agreed with the General. But there was nothing he could do about that now except hope that their anxiousness did lead to mistakes that gave away their position.

The site was guarded by four men on the top most walls, two per wall on the oddly shape structure. The only entrance was guarded by three men who were seated in old wooden chairs outside of the wrought iron gate; the chain and lock around the gate was clearly visible. Andre and Iliga would take the guards on the walls and Dimitri and Johnson would take the gate, then converge on the building to find their targets.

Their main advantage would be the complacency of the guards on the top of the building, because a normal man couldn't climb the slick, straight walls.

As soon as Andre and Iliga were off, Dimitri and Johnson made for the gate using the darkness as cover until they reached the perimeter of light. Now they waited for the distraction from the water to hide their final approach. The fishing boat that brought them in had positioned a small dinghy that would burst into flames shortly, diverting the guard's attention from the land and toward the bay.

Dimitri had insisted that they did not need the diversion because they could use their super speed to cross the final distance, but Johnson was not able to move as fast and would be a sitting target without the distraction. It was then suggested that Johnson wait at the observation position for them to return, but he quickly vetoed this idea. He wanted to observe his team.

The flames from the dinghy lit up as the ignition of the material was activated from the fishing boat. The guards turned toward the fire and everyone advanced the last hundred yards to the fortress. Dimitri did not wait for Johnson as he sped toward the gate. The guards had turned as expected to check out the flare of light and as they turned back to the front; they were face to face with Dimitri. He slashed two throats with his hands and tore into the remaining man with his fangs almost simultaneously. The last man fell to the ground as Johnson arrived, blood flowing freely from the neck where Dimitri had struck.

Dimitri leaned over one of the bleeding men and drank greedily. Johnson listened to the sickening slurping sound that he made as he drank his fill before letting the body fall to the ground with a quiet thud. Johnson watched intently as Dimitri wiped the blood from his face and licked his fingers, thinking it extremely odd the thought of eating in the middle of the mission. But this was not merely eating to the creatures, he thought, it was life and strength flowing into their bodies.

They entered into a small courtyard. Only one section was lighted; they assumed that was the location of the three targets. The dark areas contained more guards who were asleep. If things went as planned, they would kill them on the way out, leaving no survivors.

Andre and Iliga joined them and Johnson noted the similar blood stains on the their clothing which indicated that they too had fed on their prey. Hopefully they would all be focused now on the most important part of the mission, now that their thirst had been quenched...for the moment.

They approached the area that was lighted in the inside and prepared to enter through the door and window. Johnson slid up to the window and peered inside. He recognized the primary targets sitting around a table sipping drinks and playing cards; there were three other men that he did not recognize that sat away from the group. They were bodyguards. The room was oddly shaped, Johnson thought, as if sectioned off. He shrugged it off to the age of the building as he made a hand signal to Dimitri that indicated the number six. Dimitri nodded and flashed the signal to Andre and Iliga.

Dimitri indicated to Johnson that he should let them go in first, then he should follow. Johnson shook his head; he knew that the three men would not have enough time to recover before he could blanket them with his silenced automatic weapon. Johnson indicated a countdown with his fingers starting at five and working its way to one. When the last digit was gone they burst into the room.

The look of surprise on the three men sitting at the card table was not what Johnson expected to see. Realization struck them and they made to dive under the large wooden table instead of bolting from the room. Johnson levied his weapon toward them as Dimitri and his men made fast work of the bodyguards. Almost at the same moment, a false wall exploded revealing the true size of the room and three men were revealed as their weapons blazed away.

Johnson went for cover but not before being hit several times in the chest. Dimitri moved toward the armed men who smiled because they assumed they had the superior edge over the attackers. They fired a burst into Dimitri and he, in turn, smiled, as he kept moving toward them. Alarm appeared on their faces as he reached them, apparently unharmed and ripped their flesh with his clawed hands as if slicing through butter with a sharp knife.

"Take the three under the table," Dimitri growled at Andre and Iliga recognizing there was no longer a need for silence since the gunfire had erupted. "Kill them quickly," he said as he moved toward Johnson who lay on the ground unmoving.

Johnson tried to speak, but the blood pooled in his mouth making his weak words garbled and barely understandable.

"We'll get you back to the boat," said Dimitri.

"Won't...make...it," he croaked.

"The men on the fishing boat have heard the gunfire, they will move in closer to pick us up."

"I'll...be...dead by...then."

"Yes, you will," Dimitri said seeing no point in lying. "I'm sorry."

"You...you can...can...let me live," Johnson said. Dimitri watched as the blood flowed from Johnson's wounds and pooled on the ground, the smell tantalizing and teasing his senses. If not for his earlier feeding, he would not have been able to control himself.

"You so much want to be like me, don't you?"

"Yes," Johnson uttered. "Like you."

"Close your eyes," Dimitri said knowing that Johnson would soon be dead. "It may hurt for a moment but it will pass."

Johnson did as he was asked, closing his eyes under Dimitri's gaze. Dimitri placed his hands on Johnson's head and snapped his neck; Johnson uttered a brief moan and then passed.

"It is better this way," whispered Dimitri. "You have too much anger in your soul and it would be your death again and again. This way it is over, your fate sealed." He bent over and searched through the dead Lieutenant's pockets for the remote device that controlled the collars. He found it, covered in blood and shattered in the center, the result of a bullet impact. He cursed, returned it to the pocket, then picked him up the Lieutenant, slinging him over his shoulder.

"Andre, Iliga, let's go," Dimitri said as they heard the voices coming closer. "Set the explosive for thirty seconds." They removed the explosives from their packs and placed the clay-like mound and its timer on the floor.

"Out the window and head for the beach," Dimitri said. "Hurry!"

The three men moved swiftly the way they had come. A few of the hired gunmen, still putting their clothes on, crossed their path and were dispatched by Andre and Iliga who Dimitri noticed, were becoming more adept at killing. They kept a watchful eye for any explosive weapons that could harm them but at this point, saw only standard guns.

They were out the main gate as the explosion went off, lighting up the sky; sending mortar, bricks, and wood in a killing explosion from its center. They doubted if anyone inside the compound lived through it.

"WHAT THE HELL happened?" General Stone asked as he sat in the conference room at SOCOM headquarters.

"They had men hidden behind a fake wall," Dimitri said calmly. "We were in the room and committed to the fight before we could do anything. Lieutenant Johnson was in their direct line of fire. Even before I could do anything, the shots from the weapons had found him."

"Damn," the General said, "He was a good man. A lot like myself, I think," he said reflectively. Then in a sudden change of direction, his mood swung to other thoughts. "Hell, you showed them good though didn't you? Killed everyone of them."

Dimitri remained silent.

"It'll be months before they can reform into any kind of organization, and before that, we will strike again. Keep them down in their own filth of death," he said and smiled at Dimitri. "I'm not going to send you back to Norfolk yet. There is another spot I want you and your men to take care of. It will be difficult, but I'll assign another officer to take Johnson's place."

"Reese," Dimitri said, breaking his silence. "Commander Reese would be the logical choice."

"He's not an operator."

"He does not have to be. That is what went wrong last time. Johnson did not need to be in there with us. He should have waited outside the compound area. We work more efficiently without the human element, and from a distance, we can still communicate with your equipment and they can still keep tabs on what is happening. By our performance on the mission, we have proven that we can accomplish our tasks."

"Why Reese?"

"We have a rapport established and he understands our motives and behavior. And we...trust him. Anyone else you bring in at this time would be new and we would have to start fresh again, and as you have already said, time is short."

"Yes, " the General said. "Time is short and I have to admit your reasoning on Reese and the tactics make sense. You seem to be thinking with a higher level of clarity than usual."

"It's the human blood, it does that. It heightens the awareness of our minds and makes thinking sharper."

"Hmm," the General said musing. "Does that mean I shouldn't let you have too much then?"

"Do you want your missions accomplished efficiently?"

"Of course, but if you get too sharp of mind you might try and trick me."

"As long you have the power to unleash the fluid in these collars, you cannot be tricked."

"We have an understanding then."

"Oh, yes," Dimitri said. "We have an understanding."

"Good. The mission goes in two days."

REESE ARRIVED in SOCOM and was immediately taken to the area where the Team of Darkness was being kept—at the far end of the secure runway area. He found himself in the conference room waiting for General Stone, wondering what could have happened that had him summoned here on such short notice.

General Stone entered the room, Reese stood and shook hands with the man and sat back down.

"Reese, Johnson has been killed and I need you to go with the team on a mission. Can you handle that?"

"Killed how?" Reese asked. "Not by Dimitri or his men?"

"No. Gunfire from those low life drug-smuggling scum."

"I'm sorry to hear that. I liked Johnson in a way. He was a bit to gung-ho for me, but a nice enough guy. Ever since he became involved with the creatures, he seem to change somewhat, almost as if—"

"I'll be blunt with you, Reese," interrupted the General. "I need your promise to cooperate before I can explain the mission and we don't have a lot of time."

"What is the mission about?"

"All you need to know before you give me your word is that the mission is a vital part of protecting the United States from a real threat. Will you help?"

Reese said, "This is a reconnaissance mission, correct?"

"Yes. The team will go in and handle the particulars; you will monitor their progress from a remote site and guide them in and out. They will be gathering data on a group of drug lords meeting in a coastal town on Jamaica."

"Sounds simple enough."

"Good. You'll be leaving in the next couple of hours. Here is your briefing package," he said as he handed Reese a large sealed envelope. "Dimitri and his men have them already."

"Transportation?"

"Ship. The special operations patrol craft, USS Cyclone, is at dock awaiting your arrival. The majority of the crew is from the facility back in Norfolk so they are familiar with the special requirements. You load tonight and get underway immediately. Any other questions?"

"No sir," Reese answered, even though he had many questions. "I'll join the team and make preparations."

"The operation name is called Red Blood," the General added. "I'll see you when you get back. Good luck, Commander."

CHAPTER 15

Today

THE MISSION completed and the Team of Darkness safely on board the ship, Commander Reese stayed on deck as the sun began its ascension into the sky, the redness of the sunrise reminding him of the color of blood. As he thought about what had just been done, he vomited over the side of the ship.

As he tried to regain his composure, Reese realized that the time for thinking was done. He had to do something. It wasn't the deaths of the drug dealers that bothered him, but that they had been killed—without the use of the judicial system and that bothered him more. He was no fool and knew that the system was flawed, but General Stone had allowed himself to decide the fate of who lived and died.

And what about the creatures? They were now playing the role of executioner for the General in order to survive. And himself, wasn't he responsible? Had he not played an important role in devising and implementing the attack? Was that right? Could he live for the rest of his life knowing that it was he who had been the catalyst? All he had ever wanted was to study the creatures, the myth and legends in physical form right in front of him, a dream of a lifetime come true but twisted for the General's perverse crusade.

There had to be a way out of this.

What was he thinking? Was he even considering the thought of turning these creatures lose? What was the other choice? To kill them? Reese rubbed his forehead in frustration. He had two days to decide what to do; that was how long it would take to get back to the base in Little Creek.

He went below deck to check on the creatures. As usual there was a guard posted outside of the entrance to their quarters, the remote activation device securely attached to the belt. It was identical to the one that Reese had in his possession; the two-man rule was always followed.

"Everything secure?" Reese asked.

"Yes sir," the young Navy SEAL replied.

"Good," Reese said, the weariness in his voice apparent. "I'm going to get some sleep, wake me if you need anything." Reese turned and went to his stateroom. He lay on his rack, listening to the sound of the ship's engines and feeling the soothing motion of the ship as it cut through the smooth Caribbean waters. He closed his eyes and drifted off into a troubled sleep.

When he awoke, it was night and he made his way to the creature's quarters, feeling a strong desire to talk with Dimitri. He approached and was greeted by the guard and passed through into the quarters where he found Dimitri and his men sitting on their sleeping areas obviously engrossed in some kind of discussion.

"Am I interrupting?" asked Reese.

"No, come in please," said Dimitri.

Reese entered and sat in a chair that faced the three of them. Their faces appeared troubled; Reese thought that perhaps the same issues that plagued him troubled them, too.

"I see," Reese began, "you have been talking about the same subject I have been thinking about."

"And that might be what?" Dimitri asked, as his eyebrows rose.

"Putting an end to this."

"Interesting thoughts, Commander. I would like to hear your point of view on the matter."

"I do not agree with what you are being used for. I was not even aware until this mission...I assumed you were just spying on the enemy."

"The General has plans for a New World," said Dimitri.

"His plans. Not mine or even the military's for all I know. He is working on his own." Reese paused, pondering the major question in his mind.

"You want to be able to live with the decision you make."

"Yes. If you were released, then what?"

"We would go home," he said without much thought. "This is a new world, especially here in the west. In Europe, there are places that would ignore our existence as they have all these years."

"I don't know. There is another choice."

"Death?" Dimitri asked. "You will understand that we are not considering that option."

"But if you kill..."

"As we have been doing for all these years," Dimitri said interrupting him. "Have you not thought that perhaps it is part of the complete cycle of this planet or universe that creatures such as ourselves do in fact have a place in the civilization?"

"What do you mean?"

"Your Hollywood has painted us as the evil creatures that kill and destroy life. Creatures that are of the dark. We hide from the light of God and truth because we are from hell itself." He paused. "What I suggest is that perhaps we are one of God's creatures, just as yourself."

"What? That's preposterous."

"Is it now?" Dimitri asked. "Are you going to tell me that those men that we killed are not God's creatures?"

"All of man is."

"Or the animals that kill in the wild, sometimes they kill humans, too. Are these not creatures of God?"

"Yes."

"Then why is it so hard to comprehend that we ourselves are creatures of God. Put here on this Earth to play a role in the scheme of things, just as man does. We have feelings just as you do. Do we not hunger, do we not lust as you do? Do we not seek out friendship? We love, we hurt, we are happy, we are sad. Are these not feelings that you also possess?'"

"No, I don't believe all that. I can't. What of the stories? The myths and legends?"

"They are what they are. Fabrications of the period of time that they were written in to entertain and amuse those that wrote them. Were not people burned at the stake for saying or doing things that were contradictory to what was commonly called the truth or doctrine of the day?" He asked but answered his own question before Reese did. "You bet they were. So here we are, creatures that live not in accordance with the norm of the period, would we not be branded the evil denizens of hell?"

"I suppose it's possible."

"I cannot show you proof of what I am asserting, but even in your society today, prejudices still exists against those that are different in one way or another. It may not be in the depth of what it had once been, but it is still there."

"That is true," Reese conceded.

"You want proof, I have none to offer, only my beliefs of the world and the creatures within it. But then I ask you, is not religion itself only a theory? Can you show me proof that God even exists?"

"No," Reese said. "I cannot."

"So you ask me what we would do if we were released? We

would go on with our lives as we have been doing before we were discovered. Because those things make us what we are, and perhaps that is what we were meant to do all along," Dimitri said with conviction.

They sat in silence for a few moments.

"I have a plan," said Reese.

AS THE USS Cyclone was two hours from entering port under the darkness of a moonless night, Reese was on the bridge talking with the Lieutenant who was the ship's commanding officer.

"Almost home?" Reese asked.

"Yes sir," the Lieutenant answered. "Less then two hours. The current is with us, so we should—"

Three figures exploded onto the bridge, brandishing weapons. Reese stared at Dimitri and his two men as they quickly took control of the bridge.

"What are you doing?" Reese asked. "You will die for this!"

"Only if you are alive to press that button on the device you carry on your belt," Dimitri said as he held up the one that he had removed from the guard outside of their quarters. "Do you want to die?"

Reese did not answer, but his hand did not move toward the belt either.

"I didn't think so," Dimitri said as he stepped forward and removed the device from Reese's belt.

"Put the raft in the water," Dimitri said to Andre and Iliga. The two moved silently off the bridge and headed aft to do so.

"Your crew is unharmed," Dimitri began. "We did not kill anyone...yet. We will leave peaceful as long as you do not interfere with us."

"And where will you go?" asked Reese.

"That is none of your concern."

"You will be hunted down and killed."

"Maybe, but I don't think so. What is General Stone going to tell everyone, that there are vampires on the loose? I don't think so."

"But you..." Reese began.

"I'd love to talk some more, but I really must be going now." And with that Dimitri disappeared from the bridge.

As soon as he was out of sight, Reese went to his quarters and produced another device similar to the one on his belt that Dimitri had removed from him. He came back to the bridge with it where the Lieutenant was handling the ship.

"What's that?" he asked.

"Another device that he did not know about—in the event something like this would happen." He pressed the illuminated button on the device and it flashed from green to red.

"That's it," Reese said. "As soon as some of your crew is revived, we can collect the raft."

"And bodies?" the Lieutenant asked.

"There won't be any bodies," Reese said calmly and returned to his quarters.

"SUCH A WASTE," General Stone said to Commander Reese, Major Barkley, and Commander Scott as they sat around the conference table at the facility in Little Creek.

"What I can't understand is why?" Commander Scott asked. "Why did they do it if they knew it would be their deaths?"

"They didn't know about the third device on board the ship," Reese said. "They assumed that two was all there was, and before anyone else knew about the escape, they would be out of range of the device activation."

"But wasn't there a anti-tampering device built into the collars?" asked Stone.

"There was, but I believe they knew that if they were out of range long enough, the elixir would lose effectiveness and when it did, it wouldn't matter anymore if they were injected or not."

"It's over," said the General. "At least two missions were accomplished." He looked at each member around the table and said, "You all will be returned to your original units with a reminder that all of this is top secret and not to be discussed with anyone until it is, if ever, declassified."

They all nodded in understanding and were dismissed.

REESE AND Barkley gathered their things from their quarters and were awaiting the duty van to take them back to their vehicles. As they waited they talked of different things to pass the time.

"Back to Kosovo for you?" Reese asked.

"No, the General was able to get me orders back stateside. I guess it was a form of payback. You?"

"Back to my desk job right here, business as usual. I'll be retiring soon."

"That's great."

Reese heard the hesitancy in the Barkley's voice.

"What's wrong?"

"Something's bugging me."

"What's that?"

"When did you have the extra device made? I thought I had all the spares with me in medical."

"You must have missed this one," Reese said. "I have been known to have sticky fingers at times."

Barkley looked at Reese with a questioning look, and then smiled. "You Navy guys are all the same aren't you?"

"How's that?" Reese asked.

"Thieves at heart," he said and laughed. Reese laughed along with him.

"Damn, you figured me out," Reese said and clapped him on the back.

EPILOGUE

A YEAR LATER, John Reese, recently retired from the U.S. Navy was looking through the evening addition of the *Virginia Pilot* and stopped when he read the heading of an article: *Abrupt Decline of Crime in the Norfolk Ocean View Area.* As he read further, the article explained that the once crime ridden areas of Ocean View had become devoid of hardened criminal elements that had used the area as a source for numerous criminal activities. Tourism was on a healthy recovery not seen for the past twenty years. Developers were lining up to invest in the area once considered the armpit of Virginia.

This amazing turnaround of one of the most notorious areas of Norfolk was directly accredited to the police force who commented: *The hard work of the vice branch has made significant contributions to the dramatic change. The dedicated men and women of the police force have taken back their city.*

Further in the article, buried at the very end, there was an anonymous comment from a member of the force that claimed that the reduction of the crime was a result of a mysterious disappearance of the crime element and not from the direct actions of the police force.

There was no comment from the force on the remarks and they were attributed to a disgruntled employee looking to make trouble.

Reese put down the paper as he glanced toward the window. Almost sunset. He needed to get some rest. It would be a long night.

IT WAS CLOSE to midnight when Reese sat at a table in the bar called The Mad Hatter, the fourth bar he had been in this evening. It was one of several bars along the strip, an area adjacent to the Naval Station, which made it an opportune environment for drug dealers, prostitutes, and assorted others to attempt to make sales to the thousands of sailors that claimed Norfolk as their home.

"What can I get you?" asked the waitress as she placed the napkin on the table.

"How about a beer?"

"What kind?"

"Whatever you have on tap will be fine."

She hurried off to fill his order. Reese scanned the small crowd of people. He assumed it would have been more crowded for a Friday night, but not having been here before, he wasn't really sure.

"Here you go," said the waitress placing the beer on napkin. "Two bucks."

Reese gave her three.

"Thanks," she said as she gave him a friendly smile.

"Is this what you would call a normal crowd for a Friday night?"

"It was crowded earlier, during the happy hour. But the past few weeks, it has been quiet."

"Why?"

"I wouldn't want to say...but we had some bad kind of people hanging around, if you know what I mean."

"Like?"

"Oh the usual, druggies, prostitutes, drunks—you know."

"So what happened?"

"They all just...went away."

"Disappeared?"

She leaned closer to him. "I think the cops have some kind of thing going on. Like forgetting about due process and just rounding the bad guys up and taking them away like to another town or...something to get rid of them."

"I think I read about that in the paper just today."

"You believe what you read in the paper? You're a—"

"Sally," the bartender called the waitress.

"Got to get to work. Nice talking to you. Maybe I'll see you around?"

"You never know. Thanks."

Reese watched as she walked away. She was kind of cute, he thought. Maybe he would—

"Mind if I join you?"

Reese almost jumped at the voice. Not so much from the surprise of it but the fact that he recognized it. He looked in the direction of the voice and saw Dimitri.

"Have a seat. I've been looking for you."

"I know." Dimitri sat in the chair.

"How have you been?"

"Adapting."

"So it appears. I read an interesting article in the paper today."

Dimitri smiled. "Yes, I saw it, too."

"You find it amusing?"

"In a way. We have transformed a city in less than a year. We have made it safer, tourism is on the rise, and everyone is happy."

"Not everyone. What about your victims?"

"I don't think the general public would agree. They have their streets back again."

"I didn't let you escape so that you could come into where I live and kill."

"What did you expect would happen? We must survive, just as we would have if we were home. You knew that. As we did there, we prey on what society throws our way."

"Yes. I knew it. But—"

"No. Do not try and argue your conscience. We live as we have always lived throughout all these centuries. Life goes on, even for us. The only thing that has changed is our location."

"So what's next? If most of the bad people have been taken care of, what will you do?"

"As I said, we are adapting to our new environment. The article in the paper means someone has taken notice. The police believe they are responsible for the cleaning up, but eventually someone will disprove it and another explanation will be sought. It is time for us to move on before it gets to that point."

"But how? You need money here. It's not like it was in the back country of the Balkans."

"We have money. Part of our adaptation includes bank accounts, the spoils of some our clients. We have already invested in real estate all around the country."

"You certainly have become wise to our ways. So where to?"

"Somewhere," said Dimitri. "We have one more issue we need to take care of before we move."

"What?"

"It's best you don't know. And what shall you do?"

"Me? I have a book to finish."

"REESE. JOHN Reese. How the hell are you?"

"Barkley? Is that you?" Reese asked as he switched the phone to his other ear.

"Yeah it's me. I'm working on the Army staff at the Pentagon. I'm in Norfolk on business and I heard some news and thought about you so I figured I'd give you a call. How long has it been?"

"Hell, it's been about a year and a half. What news?"

"Did you hear about General Stone?"

"No?"

"They found him dead in his home yesterday."

"I figured a man like that would never die. Too damn stubborn."

"I know what you mean," agreed Barkley.

"What did he die from?"

"Are you sitting down? You're not going to believe this."

"Come on. Tell me."

"Someone drained all the blood out of him."

"What?" Reese sat down. *Why would they go after him?*

"You heard me. The blood was drained from his body."

"You mean like our friends might do it?"

"The killer tried to make it look that way. They found his blood in bottles at the killer's home."

"Damn!" said Reese. He found himself relaxing a little.

"You haven't heard the best part yet."

"What?"

"The killer was Scott. Commander Scott. They found his fingerprints at the general's home so they went to question him. They found the blood and Scott's body. He killed himself."

"Jesus Christ."

"I understand the shit is really going to hit the fan."

"Don't tell me there's more?"

"You bet. In Scott's suicide note, he said he killed Stone and then himself because he couldn't live with what they had done."

"Uh-oh. What about the Team—"

"How about we do lunch?" asked Barkley.

Reese knew he'd been intentionally cut off. "Sure. How about you come on over?"

An hour later Reese invited Barkley into his home.

"Congratulations, Lieutenant Colonel Barkley," said Reese noticing the rank insignia on Barkley's uniform.

"Thanks. It amazed me. I was junior in the selection process. I think working for the General had some fringe benefits. Either that or it was incentive to insure I kept my mouth shut."

"Nothing would surprise me anymore."

"Sorry to cut you off on the telephone like that," said Barkley.

"No. You were right. I almost slipped and said something over the phone. I should know better."

They sat in his living room exchanging pleasantries for a few moments.

"Let me get to the rest of the story. All of the files regarding our expedition into hell with the Team of Darkness are missing."

"Missing?"

"That's the term I'm using. I don't think they ever kept any to begin with."

"I think Stone probably hid more than we will ever imagine. And I don't think I want to know."

"Yeah, me too." Reese felt a sense of relief that any files pertaining to that operation were either missing or non-existing. He sensed many times that the general was operating outside of any procedures or authorizations.

"There was one other odd thing about the murder that won't make it into the press."

"What?"

"Stone's body was found wearing one of the collars I made."

"The collar? How the hell could that be?"

"I don't know where Scott got it from. I've been racking my brains over this for hours. I only made so many of those damn things. Do you have any ideas?"

"Well...no." There were no other collars, he had been sure of that. The only place that collar could have come from was Dimitri, Andre, or Iliga. Was it revenge? One of the oldest and truest acts of humanity from these creatures?

"Are you all right?" asked Barkley.

"Yeah." He tried to think of something to say that Barkley would believe. Although he liked him, he wasn't absolutely sure what he would do if he suspected the creatures were alive. "Maybe when Josip was killed, somehow Scott got hold of the collar and placed it on Stone." He said, knowing that the collar had been totally destroyed.

"That must be it. It's the only explanation that works."

"Must be it," said Reese. "Come on, let me get you a beer."

"Sounds good. So how are you occupying your time since you retired?"

"Been working on a book. For the longest time I felt I was missing something in order to finish it, a final bit of information. But now, I think I can finally put that finishing touch on it. The time feels right."

~:*~

TONY RUGGIERO

TEAM OF DARKNESS is Tony's first release by Hard Shell Word Factory. He has published numerous short stories in paper and electronic format in small press, semi-professional, and professional magazines in the science fiction, horror, and suspense genres. His other books include: *Get Out of My Mind, Mind Trap*, and *Aliens and Satanic Creatures Wanted: Humans Need Not Apply* from RFI West Publishing.

Drawing on his twenty-three years of Naval experience; where he spent four years with the Navy Seals, the idea for this book was born.

Tony was born in Irvington, New Jersey, attended college at Kean University in Union, New Jersey and then joined the United States Navy in 1978. Having spent a large portion of his Naval career in the Tidewater area, he currently resides in Suffolk, Virginia with his wife Katie, daughter Alexandra, and their Labrador retriever, Snickers.

Comments can be sent to aruggs@aol.com